Philip Davison was born in 1957 in Dublin, where he now lives. He has written three previous novels – *The Book-Thief's Heartbeat, Twist and Shout* and *The Illustrator*. He has also written television drama and, most recently, *The Invisible Mending Company*, a play for the Abbey Theatre's Peacock stage.

THE CROOKED MAN

PHILIP DAVISON

Jonathan Cape
London

First published 1997

1 3 5 7 9 10 8 6 4 2

First published in the United Kingdom in 1997 by Jonathan Cape
Random House, 20 Vauxhall Bridge Road, London, SW1V 2SA

Random House Australia (Pty) Limited
20 Alfred Street, Milsons Point, Sydney,
New South Wales 2061, Australia

Random House New Zealand Limited
18 Poland Road, Glenfield
Auckland 10, New Zealand

Random House South Africa (Pty) Limited
Endulini, 5A Jubilee Road, Parktown 2193, South Africa

Random House UK Limited Reg. No. 954009

A CIP catalogue record for this book is available
from the British Library

Papers used by Random House UK Limited are natural,
recyclable products made from wood grown in sustainable forests.
The manufacturing processes conform to the environmental
regulations of the country of origin.

ISBN 0-224-04304-8

Typeset by Palimpsest Book Production Limited,
Polmont, Stirlingshire
Printed and bound in Great Britain by
Mackays of Chatham plc, Chatham, Kent

For Joan

CONTENTS

Thanks to my editor, Robin Robertson;
thanks also to Ish and to Bob.

THERE WAS A CROOKED MAN
WHO WALKED A CROOKED MILE

I can understand that, thought Harry Fielding.
It makes perfect sense to me.

Part 1

NOT STRAIGHT

CHAPTER I

THE TESTIMONY OF
HARRY FIELDING

It has been said that in every being there is another being and this being is the true self. Not a double. Not an opposite. Simply, the one each of us strives to be all our lives. Some who have suffered cruelty, violence or abuse as children somehow short-circuit this search with their cries. They are kidnapped by the other self and abandoned in a strangely familiar place where they are victim to the same cruelty, violence or abuse, but can remember little or none of it until such time as they are strong enough to cope.

This was part of Lisa Talbot's experience of growing up. You must understand that if what follows is to make sense.

Lisa and her sister, Maureen, were assaulted and abused by their father as children. Their mother failed to protect them. She, too, was beaten. Their father was a junior banker. A money-lender to the small man. He believed everybody had their proper place in life. The fashion for the rich and royalty to appear to be like the rest of us appalled him. When he had administered a severe beating he would leave the house and seek out the company of prostitutes. Amongst them he was courteous and attentive. He would buy them drinks. On occasion, he would take one out to dinner in a cheap Soho restaurant. He would never touch them. He would secretly take satisfaction in not having to pay in full for their time. He would go home late and apologize sincerely to whomever he had beaten.

Lisa and Maureen are in their early thirties now. Their father is dead. Their mother has returned to Ireland to live with her sister.

I live next door to Lisa. Our flats are on the ground floor. We both live alone. Late one night she was startled by a man standing outside her bedroom window. It was too dark to make out his features. She knocked on my door. She was very frightened. She said he had made a menacing little whistling noise through his teeth.

This is how I came to know her. That night I went into her bedroom but, of course, the man had vanished from her window. I went outside. I saw no one. Lisa said he was probably watching from the bushes. In any case, he did not show himself again.

On the nights Maureen sought refuge in her sister's flat Lisa would spend the small hours standing in the dark thinking what she might do to protect Maureen from her violent husband. She would stand back from her bedroom window and stare out into the night as if willing the intruder to return. She would softly mimic his whistle.

I have a friend at the airport. He has a company

that loads food onto planes. He got me a job lot of dinners that come in individual foil containers. Something had gone wrong with their system and none of this batch got labelled. When I put one of these foil containers in a pot to boil I know it is going to be chicken, beef, cannelloni or curry. I do not know which. Sometimes I put two in for myself and I boil up some rice. One of these dinners tastes as good as the next if I don't think about it.

I had two of these aeroplane dinners in a pot when Lisa knocked on my door again. I was embarrassed to offer her something to eat, but I offered anyway, and she accepted. I told her I did not know what her dinner was going to be. She really did not mind. She had called to tell me she was thinking of getting a dog.

I made a fool of myself dishing out that food to her. I tried to make up for my clumsiness by flirting with her. That made me feel a bigger fool. It was not long before I was offering to look after the dog when she was away on holiday, the dog she had yet to acquire.

I eat enough for two men, but I do not get fat. When I am not overeating, I drink too much. My eyes get clouded, even swollen. When they are in this state you will see in them a mixture of shame and desire. They see small conspiracies everywhere and I applaud the conspirators. I show that I am prepared to co-operate by exhibiting all the eagerness of a coward.

I have always feared my own impulsive nature. I

have committed acts of violence in the past. I have fought with a butcher over his wife when I did not care anything for the woman. I have broken my wife's nose in my sleep. In my unconscious state I let my fist swing down hard on her face. I have taken an iron bar and smashed the car belonging to my estranged wife's boyfriend. Now, panel-beaters grin at me. Butchers regard me with suspicion. I look for a little bump on the bridge of every woman's nose.

I have got used to living on my own. There is nobody to call me selfish. If you invite me to dinner I will ask if you can cook. If the invitation still stands, I might not find your house. I blunder on, one day after the next, mostly keeping to myself. A great variety of accusations are levelled at people like me. In most instances we are innocent. We knew nobody guilty of these supposed transgressions. In most instances.

I did feel guilty about the thoughts I was having of Lisa, my neighbour. I was calculating how best I might exploit the circumstances. I had a good excuse to call. I could knock on her door to see if she was alright. I could remind her that she could call on me any time. I remember I did not eat or drink for a day when I finally decided to call on her.

She was not afraid of me. She had not closed over her bedroom door. She did not put on her shoes. I found myself earnestly fulfilling my role as good neighbour. I made a point of refusing the drink she offered. I should have brought something, I know, but I had been too busy thinking about myself before I knocked on her door.

'Tell me something about yourself,' she ventured.

'What do you want to know?' I asked.

She did not reply. She wanted a lot. I could tell. The good and the bad. What would I tell her? What did she need to know?

'What shall I tell you about myself?' she blurted out. She desperately needed to fill the silence that followed her initial request. My question did not help.

Anything, I meant to say.

'Everything,' I said stupidly. I wasn't thinking straight. This woman pulled hard on me. Nothing was clear in my head and it showed.

I began to see her regularly. She quite liked my short-order cooking and my aeroplane dinners. I had never bothered before, but now I found a way of opening and successfully resealing the foil containers. It took time, but I could tell her what she was going to get.

Then, late one night, Lisa's sister came to her again in a distressed state. Her neck was bruised. Her lip was cut. The skin around her eyes was puffy. Two nights after that Lisa got in her car and drove to her sister's house in Wandsworth. She arrived just after midnight. She parked her car in the drive that ran up by the side of the house. She went round the back. When Maureen's husband, Frank, came to the door she hit him on the side of the head with a jack handle she had taken from the boot of her car. Before he had regained his senses she tied his hands behind his back and gagged him with a cloth. She wrestled him into the back seat of her car. She struck him again with the jack handle. Now that he lay slumped on the seat she could bind his feet. She had checked just once for the unwelcome attentions of neigh-bours, then she had set about her business with grim determination. Now, she went back into the house. She filled a suitcase with his clothes and his shaving gear and put it in the boot of the car.

She had driven somewhere the night before and had returned in the small hours of the morning. This night I had followed her to the house. Now, I followed her as she drove through the streets with Frank on the back seat. I was careful to keep my distance.

She drove over Putney Bridge, went north to White City where she took the Westway. She got into lane and kept a steady speed. I got in behind her. I was thinking about what she had told me of her father over our in-flight dinners. She had described the beatings and the abuse matter-of-factly.

I kept a steady speed and I watched for Frank's head surfacing in the back window of her car, but he remained crumpled on the seat.

She did not stay on the motorway long. It was dangerous for her. She might have to stop to hit her brother-in-law again with the jack handle. She got off the motorway at Beaconsfield. There was very little traffic once we were clear of the town. The roads got narrower. I fell further behind. Only now, in a darker environment, was I aware that the moon shone above us. It was an unusually mild night.

The air was uncomfortably thin. That moon looked heavy, like it might fall out of the sky.

I caught myself making that whistling noise through my teeth. I switched on the car radio, but could not tune in satisfactorily. The chimes of Radio Moscow were coming through.

Some way beyond Beaconsfield she got lost. I was forced to follow without headlights as she travelled a network of third-class roads that traversed a wooded area. She was looking for one particular turning, a foresters' gate, a track.

It was three and three-quarter hours from the time she left the house in Wandsworth to the time she found the clearing in the wood she had selected. She had had to stop the car to strike Frank a third time on the head with the jack handle.

The track from the road swung in a wide arc and split into several routes. She took the one with a steep incline. This led to the clearing. I was some way behind. I parked half a mile away, near the gate, but off the main track. She would be leaving before me. I did not want her seeing my car. The trees were densely packed. Fortunately, there was not much undergrowth. I was able to cut across through the trees. The canopy above did not allow the moon to light the forest floor. It was difficult to remain on my feet as I advanced over the uneven ground. There were many dips and hollows. I had to take my time. She was on a plateau of sorts. There was a ridge that obscured her car but I had the spill light from her headlamps as my beacon.

When I eventually had covered enough ground to allow a clear, close view, I found that she had already dragged him out of the car. His hands and feet were still bound. He was caught in the headlights. I heard him moan. He rolled onto his side as she quickly moved away from him. He got no closer than one-half a body width to the line of trees that marked the edge of the clearing. The gag in his mouth appeared to make his eyes bulge. For a moment I thought our eyes connected. Then, Lisa drove over him. She travelled back and forth over his body four times. I watched her bury him with his suitcase in a grave she had dug the previous night when she had found this place. I watched her get back into her car and reverse down the track.

I stayed crouched where I was for some considerable time, staring into the dark where she had buried him. I moved when I thought it was safe to move. I stepped out into the moonlight that bathed the clearing and showed the way down the track. It began to rain. I could hear it raining in the trees, but it was not raining on me. Not in this clearing. Not on the track before me. There were no clouds that I could see. The moon hung in a clear black sky.

I opened my dry mouth and drew a deep breath. I began the walk to my car. I kept to the track. It was a shorter distance than I had thought.

How far ahead had she planned? How often did Frank go on a trip and leave his car in the garage? I was sure Lisa had not confided in her sister. She had done it all on her own. For her build she had found extraordinary physical strength, and she had had the presence of mind required to carry out the deed. Had she buried him deep enough? Had she laid the suitcase across his chest? Did she know that the forest floor moves? In time, it bulges, it gives way. Like the sea, it tends to return a body.

It was dawn when I drove down Marylebone Street. The chimes of Radio Moscow were ringing in my head.

The curtains in Lisa's bedroom were drawn shut.

I was a little drunk when I knocked on her door at about six o'clock the following evening. I had a bottle of whiskey which was three-quarters full under one arm. I had a grubby old shoe I pulled out from under my wardrobe in one hand. I thrust the bottle into her hand.

'That's for you,' I said, my eyes narrowing. Then I thrust the shoe on her. 'That's for the dog,' I said.

It was for the dog she had not yet bought.

'You're a mess,' she said. There was disdain in her voice, but no surprise. Perhaps she had put her ear to the wall and had heard the neck of the bottle collide with the rim of my glass too many times to be surprised.

'I feel great,' I barked. My eyes had suddenly widened, but they must have been cloudy. They wandered a moment then fixed on Lisa's face. Her hands were full. That cleared the way for me to take hold of her small pink ears. I pulled hard on her ears thinking I might stretch that scowl off her face. 'Just great,' I said.

She did not like my patronizing her. She pulled away forcefully. She had been drinking, too. I had seen her sister leave earlier and now Lisa was panicking on her own.

'What do you want from me?' she asked fiercely.

I did not know now what I wanted from her. I only knew I felt very close to her at that moment. I felt uneasy, yes, but not as before when I had found it difficult to look into her eyes.

I told her I wanted to take her to dinner.

We got into my car. I asked her where she wanted to go. She deliberately misunderstood me. She told me she wanted to learn Italian. She wanted to go and live in Italy, if she could find somebody to go with her.

Do not confuse me with your fantasies, I wanted to say, give me the facts you conceal. Confirm what I have seen with my own eyes. I will listen carefully and I will understand.

We drove to Chinatown. The damn car can find its way there by itself.

We had dinner upstairs in a place I frequent. The grandmother was in charge on this floor. She had her youngest son, her niece and her daughter-in-law working out of the dumb waiter. Beside the service counter there was a heavy curtain hung across a doorway. Behind the curtain there were five Chinese children in pyjamas playing on a blanket on the floor. They had building blocks, plastic toys, paper and coloured chalk. They were quiet, but once in a while a little flat face would push through the folds in the curtain and granny would chase the child back behind the curtain with a surly frown. Evidently, the old woman enjoyed this.

We took a corner table. I sat with my back to the wall. Lisa sat facing me. I had a clear view of the stairwell over her shoulder. The service counter and the curtained den were to one side.

Lisa had not eaten that day. She was hungry. She ordered beef in blackbean sauce. I ordered prawns and I ordered chicken and Singapore fried noodles and a pot of green tea. I put a lot of soya on the noodles. I craved salt. We both crammed the food into our mouths. Before my eyes Lisa seemed to replenish her strength. I tried to keep pace with her. All the time I was thinking ahead. Thinking I would have to get out of Chinatown to get a strong coffee. As soon as I had finished eating I would crave caffeine. A double espresso would see me right. Then, I might have a drink. It seemed to me it had been a long time since I had had a drink. I was thinking Lisa and I might go to a dive her father frequented.

I needed to prove to myself that in spite of the closeness I felt I was not hopelessly entangled in this woman's life, that she had no hold on me. I fixed on the young woman behind the counter. She was the daughter-in-law. Her demeanour made me think she believed that two strangers might meet and make each other happy regardless of the circumstances. Either that, or she had the presence of mind and the skill to pick any pocket she pleased with her long, slender fingers. Those fingers reached to the tips of the pair of large rubber gloves she wore to wash dishes. She was tall. She was an inch taller than me. She had to stoop to get her hands to the bottom of the sink beneath the high counter. She was working faster than I was stuffing food into my mouth with my sticks. I could not keep up with her, either. I decided it would be easy to fall in love with her. She seemed to promise that she would remain a stranger however often I kissed her lips, however often her hands might caress me.

I choked. She kept washing. Lisa poured me some green tea. Lisa and I then made polite conversation, as lovers do to mock their intimacy. Her fearless streak was again evident.

We all pretended that everything was normal, or rather, that each of us was in control. They were short-staffed that night. Somebody was out sick. The old woman was giving her daughter-in-law a hard time. She publicly admonished her with the same few repeated phrases until the young woman answered back. That really got the old woman's goat. She began a tirade. I interrupted my eating and made a point of looking down my nose at her. I muttered bad-temperedly. I tapped on our teapot with my sticks until I got her attention. Lisa was alarmed by my action.

The old woman stopped haranguing her daughter-in-law long enough to look at me uncomprehendingly. Then, she started again.

'Ah, for God's sake,' I wailed, 'let her be.'

Other customers in this small dining room let out little nervous noises or widened their eyes at each other. They were only prepared to glance at the rowing women. My friend behind the counter was giving as good as she got. The old woman's son kept clear. He took his time clearing a table in the opposite corner. It was his elder brother's wife at the sink. Had his brother not rung in sick she would not have had to suffer and he was going to tell his brother as much when he saw him at the card table later that night.

The old woman's niece was braver. She tried to intervene, but was quickly rebuffed. She summoned her uncle by singing a sorry song into the dumb waiter shaft.

'Leave us all in peace, for God's sake,' I whined, 'we've had enough.' My voice did not carry.

The two women were shouting at each other now. The young one was in tears but she kept washing the dishes. The old man appeared at the top of the staircase. His slight, bony figure only half filled his starched white shirt. He was a wiry little man with a cigarette in his mouth and a severe squint. Evidently, his squint was not severe enough to intimidate his wife. He tried using a conciliatory tone and when that made no impression he put his hands on his hips and delivered a firm rebuke. He was disgusted with his wife's behaviour, but not surprised by it. Ordinarily he was a match for her, but he was not prepared to add to the scene in front of customers. The old woman got him back down the stairs with a few belligerent words. There was peace for a short time. The children who had come out to watch the row develop were ushered back behind the curtain. The old woman apologized to one party who made a point of leaving the restaurant, then she started again.

I was drawn into this domestic scene. I was gladly involved. It soothed me. However, the dispute had the opposite affect on Lisa. Suddenly, she had to get out. The food was not sitting right in her stomach. Forget the espresso. We would go straight to a bar.

I got up and interrupted the old woman's new tirade with my demand for the bill.

'Yes, sorry,' she said. 'Sorry, you know.' She indicated her daughter-in-law, then she gave me our bill.

I smiled sympathetically at the young woman behind the counter, but my attentions seemed not to register with her. She was too distraught. Too busy washing dishes in the sink.

The old woman was now making a public apology behind my back. 'Sorry. Sorry, you know,' she announced to the remaining customers.

Lisa would not let the young man help her with her coat. She took it from him and thrust her arms into it.

At last, the young woman looked at me. I smiled again and felt foolish. She was distracted by the two men ascending the staircase. I turned in time to catch sight of the two Special Branch detectives as they reached the top of the stairs. I knew what they were immediately. I was sure they had come for Lisa. I pushed her through the curtained doorway.

This doorway led nowhere. There was no exit. No window. No fire escape. Lisa and I stood among the quiet children. I looked hard into her eyes and she into mine. The two detectives stepped through the curtain. The old woman followed, protesting fiercely.

It had not taken long for Frank to surface. Someone's dog had dug him up. Somebody had seen my car at the scene of the crime. A copper had spotted my car parked in a lane in Chinatown. Armed detectives had been sent. They had come for me.

On the way out, I told the old woman she was not looking after her grandchildren. If there was a fire, I told her, they would be burnt alive.

CHAPTER 2

ABOUT HARRY

I have recounted to you what I told the police. Naturally, they wanted to know why I did not move to prevent her from killing her brother-in-law. I told them that I could not give a satisfactory answer to that question. I could only say that it was as if she was doing it to protect me. Frank was a thug who was getting a little more than he deserved. I could live with that.

It had been an ill-conceived act on Lisa Talbot's part. I told the police that had I intervened it would have been to make a better job of it. Naturally, that gave them the hump.

I have told you Lisa Talbot's story to show that my world is the real world. Lisa and I are two of a kind. We have not found the strength to cope with the damage that has been done to us in the past. Neither of us has any sympathy for the children we once were. Our energies are devoted to defending ourselves and others here and now. We seek to protect, but we are cowards. We mark our targets early, when they first threaten us. We hit hard and run. We are capable of grievous harm.

I realize that I have singularly failed to protect Lisa Talbot. It is as if I have betrayed her. The irony of my having led to her arrest scores my hardened heart.

Furthermore, I was seen to be careless and that leads me now to explain something of my job. Let me give you an account of a very different dinner engagement. When I have dinner with Hamilton, my boss, it is usually at a motorway stop. Call it dinner, call it breakfast. We usually meet in the small hours. My boss is an influential man. He arranged for me to be cleared of any charges in respect of the Lisa Talbot case. I could have been charged with failing to report a serious crime. They might even have pressed for a charge of conspiracy. Hamilton wasn't performing a benevolent act. He would have let me stew had he not wanted me for a job. As it was, he had to send his little message through his network of masonic civil servants to ensure that his name could not be linked with mine.

When politics or circumstances dictate that extra caution is prudent Harry Fielding can be called upon to break into a solicitor's office or the house of a politician. He can act as bodyguard, secure premises for a clandestine meeting or for the purpose of blackmail. He can launder money. He can administer a beating. He can pick a fight. As a rule chaps from the firm don't get into fights. On the rare occasions that they do they like to have a little chat first. Some point of history perhaps, or some philosophical debate. It helps them get their bearings. They can work down from there. Harry can spy on any member of the firm whose private life is cause for concern. There is no kidnapping. No killing. Chaps do that. I am called variously: villain, criminal, bob-a-job man, by those whose job it is normally to undertake such tasks. Understrapper is the official term used to describe me. There are others who do the same job, though I have met none. We are domestic animals. We rarely get to travel abroad on business. We don't get paid expenses. Ours is contract work without the contract. We can be safely denied within the firm as well as externally. At MI6 operatives are told that they are in the business of creating myths. At MI5 they are told that they are defending the realm. Harry Fielding is told to meet Hamilton at 2.00 a.m. in a motorway cafeteria.

I'm not complaining. I do my job well and they pay promptly. I'm ambitious. I want promotion. I think that is why Hamilton mocks me.

If it can be avoided they will not issue an understrapper with equipment of any kind. Understrappers are never furnished with guns. If I want to carry a weapon, Hamilton tells me, I must purchase one in the market place. I haven't signed the Official Secrets Act. There is nothing official about me.

Unless it is bodyguard work (and this kind of work is rare) mugs like me are discouraged from carrying a weapon. This involves a certain amount of hypocrisy on their part. That, of course, makes me feel better if I choose to carry a loaded pistol on any other kind of job. That is to say, without actually encouraging me, the firm cultivates the notion that I always know best when it comes to judging circumstances in the field, irrespective of the amount of information they are prepared to give me.

I tell Hamilton I don't take jobs that require a gun, but I carry a Beretta anyway. This Beretta was made in 1934. The man who sold it to me wanted to sell me a larger, more powerful pistol that carries thirteen instead of the seven this one holds. I took the seven-shot model. I'm no gangster. I wanted something compact. I told him I didn't think anybody's skin had grown thicker since 1934. If I ever had to use it it would be to discharge no more than two shots at close range.

Hamilton knows I carry it. His refusal to acknowledge my needs is part of the game.

I no longer look at the world with that fixed, confident stare of youth. Instead, my eyes hunt for the telling detail. I try to match what I pick out with experience. I invent the rest. This can be dangerous.

I could see from the way Hamilton was sitting that I had incurred his displeasure. I had been careless and I had been stupid. There could be no excuse for my behaviour. As usual, he had selected a booth with a clear view of the entrance. Without having to reveal myself I could observe him stiffly perched in one corner of the seat. He was well turned out in his three-piece suit. He had shaved before coming out to meet me. He had a newspaper spread neatly before him on the table. I was already late. I decided I would let him sit. No harm to get his blood pressure up a little further if I could manage it. I went back to my car. I sat in the front passenger seat for another thirty minutes. I sang a song to myself. I thought about Hamilton's smooth face. When Hamilton shaved before coming out to meet at 2.00 a.m. it meant his blood pressure was already up. I imagined on such nights he had his instructions for the week and a car boot full of money.

He had the use of several different cars. That night he had come in the green Rover 2000. It was parked in a space near the exit ramp. I fancied this was his own car.

2.45am. It was time to eat. Hamilton has never eaten breakfast cereal in his life. Kippers are more his line. Kippers at the club. I bought three of those fairy boxes of cornflakes, a jug of milk, a pot of coffee. I got them to add two spoonfuls of instant coffee to the pot to make it stronger. This kept me at the counter for quite some time. When I sat down opposite Hamilton he was still able to pretend that he was happy to see me. Some of Hamilton's pretences are short-lived.

'Did I get you out of bed?' he asked with a sneer.

'No,' I said, 'I didn't quite get as far as the bed.'

I ripped open two of the three boxes and poured their contents into my dish. I poured my coffee. I poured the milk.

'Damn.' I had forgotten the sugar. I got up to go for some sugar. 'Do you want anything up there?' I asked.

'Hamburger and chips,' he said. His sneer had suddenly given way to an impish grin.

'You devil you,' I said. He would have flushed with naughty delight had he not been secretly angry at my being late. He had refrained from eating until my arrival. This strategy suggested that he had arrived only a few minutes earlier himself.

Let people indulge themselves, I say. Don't deprive them. I can't pass a drunk on the ground without getting him up on his feet and propping him in some doorway. If he has a bottle I put it in his hand.

I got Hamilton his hamburger and chips. I made him give me the exact money. I brought back three sachets of sugar and sprinkled their contents on my cornflakes.

I wasn't going to thank him for helping me out and he knew better than to expect my gratitude. He had all the details he needed of the Lisa Talbot case. For all the 'disappointment' he expressed at my carelessness and my clumsiness, something in his tone suggested that he drew satisfaction from my involvement in the matter. I had indulged Lisa Talbot in a heinous act. Sympathy is most often shared fear or shared anger. The firm operates on the basis that anybody can be put to good use if it can be established what it is that fuels their anger and their fear. It's a fair assumption.

As I shovelled the cornflakes into my mouth I recognized that somehow, Hamilton's hand had been strengthened.

When it came to reproaching me Hamilton did

not refer directly to the Lisa Talbot case. Instead, he got on his hobby-horse. With his index finger he tapped the newspaper that remained spread under our plates. It was to be found in here, he told me – there was a new and sinister confidence evident. One only had to read any of the increasing number of reports of villains being poisoned in restaurants or shot dead in their hospital beds. Reports of murderers transporting the bodies of their victims in wheelbarrows through built-up areas. Reports of parents of children killed by drunk drivers taking savage revenge. Even the stories in the skin magazines featured vigilante heroes.

I told him not to believe everything he read in the newspapers. They were now printing photographs that had been doctored by computers. Soon, all press photographers would be using digital cameras. There would be no negatives to check the authenticity of an image, no way of determining what was original. It would fit him better to worry about that.

Hamilton likes to describe himself as the queen's messenger. What the hell can you expect from a man like that? Hamilton and his kind don't give a damn whether or not the politicians place the firm on a statutory basis. The line between policing and intelligence work is becoming increasingly blurred. A new regime is already in place. In this new regime problems are defined by the same old hands, of course, but they are being filed in different compartments. Budgets are being scrutinized ever more closely. More effort now goes into the concealment of real costs and the secretion of special funds. There is more contract work. More understrappers operating. This makes the whole operation more cost effective. In this new age of transparency there is more scope for mystery and confusion.

The secret service, the Freemasons, the Oddfellows, the Knights of Columbanus, the Orange Order, Opus Dei, sooner or later these legends will appear in brackets after people's names listed in the telephone directory. I told Hamilton this before. I asked if he thought they might let us both remain ex-directory.

So, what did the queen want with me at 3.00 a.m. that particular morning? She wanted me to spy on one of her cabinet ministers.

Cabinet ministers have to be protected, even when they are out cheating on their wives. If a cabinet minister is out cheating on his wife he doesn't want to bring his Special Branch bodyguards with him. He tries to give them the slip. He is happier knowing that they are guarding his wife and children while he is making his visit. If the jolly coppers know about his little ploy some new faces are drafted to cover those visits. As a matter of course they bring their expensive camera equipment and take some photographs. Taking account of these additional man hours it would appear that more tax-payers' money is spent protecting the male cabinet minister than the female cabinet minister. She is either more faithful, or she is more cunning in conducting her affairs. If, however, the jolly coppers are not aware of our man giving them the slip, he continues to be protected at the cheaper rate.

Hamilton is in a position to hear about such affairs. His tentacles have a long reach. Officially, he is a lowly civil servant working for the Joint Intelligence Committee which operates out of the Cabinet Office. When he isn't busy meeting people like me he is responsible for bringing together and presenting information from the different services. Hamilton serves more than one queen. He can poo-poo any suggestion that a politician be put under surveillance because of gossip or rumour. He can then put me on the job. Somebody the Special Branch won't recognize. I, too, am told to bring my camera (a very much cheaper model). There is no such thing as a bit of useless information if you have a good filing system.

I topped up my sodden cornflakes with my third box. Hamilton wouldn't give me details until he had finished eating. Eventually, he put his knife and fork to rest and carefully draped his used napkin over what remained on his plate. Then, reluctantly it seemed, he gave me the information I needed. He wanted pictures.

The following night I was parked on the corner of a narrow street in Islington watching an upstairs window. The air was thick with pollen spores. I was hoping it would rain. Rain would clear it. Wash the stuff down the drains. I had taken a strong anti-histamine and it was making me giddy. I didn't want to have to take any more of them.

Our man wasn't due that night. I wanted to reconnoitre. I wanted to work out the geography of her flat. I wanted to be able to identify her neighbours. I had arrived there mid-afternoon. It was now eleven o'clock at night. There was nothing left in my flask. I had bought a bag full of health food snacks. These snacks were gone. Little bits of nut were stuck between my teeth.

His mistress's flat was in a house on the end of a terrace. I was particularly interested in the back of the house. There was a small door in an eight-foot wall that led from the back garden into the side street where I was parked. I had been around the block twice on foot, once in each direction. I had been told that our man came and went by the door in the garden wall. I could catch him on his way in and on his way out. To get photographs through the bedroom window I would have to get up on the roof of the house abutting hers. That would be difficult.

I plotted my route. I would have to scale a wall at the far corner of the block. The adjacent street was a busy street. I might have to wait some time for my opportunity. Then, I would have to cross a fragile corrugated roof with a steep slope. Then, I had to climb a short length of drainpipe. Most difficult of all was to get myself from the top of the drainpipe over the gutter and onto the roof. It might take fifteen minutes or more to get into position.

Some of those gutters looked unsafe. I didn't want to do it twice. To hell with a trial run.

*　　*　　*

Angela. That was her name. The next day I followed her to work. She was a film editor. The cutting rooms were in the West End. I sat outside the premises for much of the day. She kept irregular hours. We had lunch together at three in the afternoon, though she was unaware of our association. I sat across the room from her.

She ate a lot of sweet things. To compensate, she ate a salad sandwich without dressing. I could tell she didn't much like salad sandwiches. I could see her eating health food together with chips and ice-cream.

She was an attractive, confident woman. She had a system for eating. I got the impression from watching her that she would undertake a task only if she could bring her skills to bear. She caught me looking at her once. It didn't bother her. She was comfortable with her secret.

You can ring around the cutting rooms of any city at ten o'clock at night and chances are you'll get an answer if they have work. Angela packed up early that night. She left at 8.30 p.m. She went to a grocery shop near her flat. She bought food. Our man was coming to supper.

By 9.30 p.m. I was in position on the roof. He had arrived on foot. Most likely he had taken a taxi to the district and walked the last part of his journey. I had photographed him passing through the wall via the small door. He had his own key.

The bedroom and the kitchen were at the rear of the house. The bedroom window was partially screened by the branches of a lime tree. There was just enough glass clear for me to operate.

From what I had learnt of Angela watching her earlier that day I had judged her to be thorough. I had expected she would have closed the bedroom curtains as a matter of routine before he arrived. This night, however, she was flustered. She hadn't left the cutting rooms early enough. I watched her hurry with the preparations for supper. She was distracted. She was bothered. She didn't want him over tonight. She burnt her finger. It was my good fortune she neglected to draw the bedroom curtains.

No doubt, one or other of them would draw the curtains if they were going to go to bed together. I might just catch them together in the bedroom before they did so.

It hadn't rained in the city for two months. The pollen count was high. In spite of the pills I had a bout of sneezing up on that roof. Stifling it made the muscles in my neck lock.

I took ten shots of them together in the kitchen. Angela wouldn't keep still. She kept getting up from her chair and pacing the small floor space available to her. He kept getting in the way. Then, she left the kitchen. He followed. Perhaps they entered the living room, or she went to the bathroom, or they stood in the hall. All I could do was wait.

I could hear a radio in the room directly beneath me. I could hear a baby crying in the adjacent house. The smell of garlic drifted up from the kitchen below and mingled with smoke from a chimney

29

stack halfway along the terrace. These were cold summer nights. Because my muscles were tense my body would not hold heat.

Hamilton sends me out on this kind of job when he can satifactorily concoct the image he wants on a computer. He can illustrate a truth as readily as a lie. He won't do it. It's not acceptable. But soon, he won't be able to resist.

I shivered. I wasn't paying full attention to my task. I was thinking about Lisa Talbot and what she had done in the woods. I remembered wanting to reach out into the dark. I should have shown myself. I should have dug the hole deeper for her.

Suddenly, I didn't want to watch people any more. I was sick of it. Then, a little voice in my head said, 'Make it more exciting. Get closer. Climb that tree. Listen to what they are saying on the other side of the glass. Listen to the little noises they make.'

Then, something happened in another room. A standard lamp was knocked over. Angela re-emerged in the kitchen. When he entered the kitchen she had a steak knife in her hand. They were shouting at each other. He wrenched the knife from her. She reached for something else. He stabbed her in the heart.

My finger dropped repeatedly onto the button – my thumb wound on repeatedly to the end of the roll. I didn't know what I was getting. What a world.

My head was spinning. Suddenly, the smell of garlic made me gag. Then, I felt the rage build in me.

I made my way along the terrace roofs as quickly as I dared. I got down onto the slanted corrugated roof, then I had to wait. There was a couple kissing beside a parked car.

When I got to the side street where my car was parked I dumped the camera under the front seat. I threw the safety catch on the Beretta. I keep a pair of thin, black cotton gloves under the dashboard. With these I can get my finger on the trigger and have a little space spare. I pulled on the gloves as I walked towards the door in the wall.

It had taken me some seven or eight minutes to get that far. I expected that our man would have left by now. I was sure that a politician would take the time to close all doors behind him, however appalling the circumstances. Sure enough, the door in the garden wall was shut. The lock was worn, difficult to pick. I climbed the wall.

It seemed none of the neighbours had been disturbed. There was nobody peering out of any of the windows. I picked the lock on the back door. In splitting the house into flats this had been made a private entrance.

It was warm inside. I caught the smell of sweet aromatic oil as I ascended the narrow staircase.

I found her on the kitchen floor. She had moved from where she had fallen. He was still there with her. He was sitting on a chair with his legs apart and his head in his hands. I was standing right behind him before he was aware of my presence. He sprang to his feet when he saw me. He nearly fell over her. He put his fists to either side of his head. He backed himself against the open door. There were little flecks of spittle on his chin. He was in a state of shock.

'Who are you?' he asked in a small, even voice. Somehow he knew I wasn't a friend.

I didn't answer. I looked at Angela on the floor, this woman I had known for a day. He had removed the knife. She was no longer angry. Were it not for the blood it would have appeared that she was sleeping with her eyes open, sleeping in a comical position. She was missing a shoe. That was in one corner of the kitchen.

I bent down. I felt for the pulse in her neck. There was no pulse.

'Who are you?' he asked again. This time there was more confidence in his voice.

I got up and I slapped his face, this man I was used to seeing on the six o'clock news. I slapped him hard. It got him thinking again in some kind of primitive way.

'Where's the knife?' I asked.

He indicated a drawer. He had pulled the steak knife out of Angela's heart and had put it in the drawer with the other knives. People do things like that.

He went to get it. He had washed the blade. He may or may not have wiped the handle clean of prints. Now, he didn't know which damn steak knife it was. I scooped the lot out of the drawer. I ordered him to get his coat and get down the stairs.

'Are you Special Branch?' he asked.

I just stared at him until he moved. He stepped

over her to get his coat without looking down. He had made a conscious decision not to look at Angela again.

I led him to my car. I put him in the front passenger seat. I swear to God, had he run I would have caught him and beat him. In the event, he did exactly as I asked. It was as if I had come to save him, and maybe I had. I didn't know what I was going to do, but I had decided I would get him away from that place as quickly as possible.

He didn't speak again until we were well clear of the neighbourhood.

'Where are you taking me?' he asked.

His voice was so familiar, so reassuring. His words were little darts that made me jump.

'I'll drop you near your house. Give me the address.'

He gave me his address. 'What will happen then?' he asked.

'That's not for me to say.'

'You haven't told me who you are.'

'I'm the tooth fairy.'

'Damn you,' he said. He reached down under the dashboard and began to rummage among some papers I keep there. Nothing with personal information on it.

'Don't distract me,' I told him, 'I'm on medication.'

He didn't need me to tell him just how vulnerable he was at that point. He shoved the papers back where they belonged.

'What will you do now?' he asked.

'I'll make a call. You won't be needed.'

Suddenly, his composure cracked.

'Oh God, what have I done?'

'You've killed a woman, sir. You've stabbed her with one of the knives I've got in my pocket.'

'You don't understand.'

'I understand.'

'She made threats. Oh my God, what have I done? Stop the car. Pull over. I have to think.'

'You should have done that before you stuck a knife in her heart.'

He said nothing to this. He stared straight ahead. Traffic was light. We were having an easy passage through the lighted streets.

'Killed her . . .' he finally echoed. Then he turned on me sharply. 'Maybe you're wrong. Maybe she's not dead. We must go back.'

I slapped his face again.

He was quiet for a moment, then he began to sob.

'Don't talk to anybody about this,' I warned. 'Nobody.'

Not once had he looked behind him or glanced in my far wing mirror. He was thinking ahead. He was trying to make plans. He turned on me again. He studied me closely, committing my features to memory.

'What are you going to do?' he demanded.

'Nobody,' I repeated. 'That includes me, pal.'

What *was* I going to do? I hadn't yet decided. I

was remembering the look Angela gave me when she caught me staring at her at lunchtime. I was thinking about her eating a salad sandwich because it was good for her. I was thinking about the roll of film in the camera under the cabinet minister's seat.

A fine rain began to fall. It wasn't enough to allow the windscreen wipers a smooth sweep. It wouldn't be enough to clear the air.

Chapter 3

THE DEEP HOLE

He would not forget my face. I had had a long, hard look at him, too. Driving the cabinet minister away from the scene of the killing opened my eyes to a few unpleasant facts about myself. Secretly, I revelled in the power that lay within my grasp. I was protecting a powerful man *and* I had that roll of film in the camera under his seat. I was, by any measure, a success. What did I feel for the woman who lay dead on her kitchen floor? I can say that at that moment I felt nothing. The man sitting next to me understood this and, consequently, he feared me.

I was aware that I was involved in a momentous miscarriage. I would not be able to stand outside it as I had done in the case of Lisa Talbot. The hole I was digging as we drove through the lighted streets was already too deep. I could not get out. I knew that I would sleep that night, but not rest. I would wake in the morning to find I had been digging in my sleep and that I would see no way out.

I didn't want to use the cellular phone. It wouldn't be safe, not even for the cryptic message I was going to give Hamilton. The job, after all, was supposed to have nothing to do with the firm. I stopped at the first call box I saw. I telephoned Hamilton. That is, I rang the number he had given me in case of emergency.

'I must speak with Mister Hamilton,' I told the voice at the other end of the line, 'it's urgent. Barrett is the name.'

'Mister Hamilton will return your call. Has he the number, Mister Barrett?'

'I'm in a call box.' I dictated the number.

'Wait,' said the voice. Then the line went dead. I put down the receiver.

It was the usual cut-out routine. Hamilton would know the name Barrett. It was he who had given it to me. Barrett was my 'commercial' name. Yes, it was a basic security precaution, but it was also a title given to flatter – a little extra mystique instead of a little extra money. It was an honour bestowed on those who were deemed to be one notch above the common criminal. Naturally, Hamilton didn't like my using it. Using it was his prerogative. When I used the name Barrett it meant trouble.

Hamilton rang from a call box a short time later.

'Well?'

'Our man is in trouble. You'll want to meet me immediately.'

'Will I?' came the frosty response.

We met in Camden. I was at the appointed spot before Hamilton. He pulled his car into the kerb a few yards up from mine. I got into his front passenger seat. I told him what I had seen and done. I told him our man had stuck a steak knife bearing Her Majesty's crest into Angela's heart, and that I had driven him home. I told him everything except that I had a full roll of pictures to be developed.

He, of course, asked about photographs.

'Ten shots of them together in the kitchen,' I told him, 'before anything happened.'

I held back on the others because I had a bad feeling – with something this big somebody somewhere might say, 'Witness? What witness?' A few incriminating photographs might save my life.

I knew by the way Hamilton was avoiding my eyes that he did not believe me. I knew that sooner or later he would ask for the unbroken roll of negatives. What the hell. I wouldn't give it to him until it suited me. I'd let him sweat along with me.

'Pity you didn't get it all,' he said. 'Still, you've done well.'

He pretended he wasn't shocked by the news of the killing. In any case, he soon recovered. He rang someone from his car phone. He got the minister's number. He rang the minister, addressed him by his first name, introduced himself, told him not to worry.

He was taking a calculated risk. In Hamilton's mind events of whatever magnitude or complexity invariably boiled down to disaster or triumph. There was no doubt in his mind which this was going to be. Things were in hand, he told the minister. 'Our friend,' he said referring to me, 'is looking after everything.'

Hamilton's righteous yet familiar tone was truly

chilling. With this one brief phone call he had effectively demonstrated that he was the power-broker. He was in control. Both the minister and I would be needing his help and his guidance.

To start with, he was going to help me dispose of the body 'if,' as he put it, 'the body hadn't yet been tampered with.'

I left my car parked on the street in Camden. Hamilton drove us to a lock-up garage in Spitalfields. The garage was cold and damp. There was a smell of rotten wood and oil. This smell mingled with the smell of fish which came from somewhere else. There was one sixty-watt bulb for illumination. There was a large factory clock on the wall that kept the right time. There was a brass tap that had been screwed so tightly onto the head of the pipe that rose out of the ground, it sat at an angle of forty-five degrees. The washer inside was worn. The tap dripped into a gully that had no grating.

In this garage there was a blue transit van with twelve hundred miles on the clock. It had a full tank of petrol. It had one of those air-freshener balls on the floor.

I had not been in this place before. Hamilton let us in with his own key. He knew where to look for the keys to the van. They were kept in the exhaust pipe. He had to use a length of stiff wire to fish them out.

It was just after midnight. As we drove to Islington Hamilton questioned me on the geography of the flat and the conditions we could expect. I described the relative position of windows and doors. I told him which lights had been left on. I described the cover foliage afforded on the short journey from the door at the back of the house to the door in the garden wall.

He repeated each observation I made.

'It's on the kitchen floor?' he asked.

IT, not *she*. This was meant to make our job easier. This somehow emphasized the speed at which we would need to work. This was the second time he had asked the question.

'Yes.'

'What does it weigh?'

'Christ . . .'

'What does it weigh?' he repeated.

'I don't know – nine stone . . .'

Before leaving the garage Hamilton had loaded a body bag and cleaning utensils and materials into the back of the van. He had pulled these things out of an oil drum. I glanced at these items now. *20p off your next purchase* read one label.

I wound down my window. The smell of air freshener was making me ill.

'Getting it into the van,' said Hamilton, 'that's the dangerous part.'

He kept a constant speed. Traffic lights seemed synchronized to facilitate our passage. Lisa Talbot had driven at this speed and I had kept pace. Killers and their associates, it seemed, made responsible motorists. This was the speed at which one drove to hell, not at ninety miles an hour, as many thought.

We made two passes in the van. We could see no suspicious vehicles, no plain-clothes detectives, no sign of surveillance. We parked in the same narrow street where I had previously parked. Hamilton pulled the van in as close to the door as he could get.

Everything appeared to be as I had left it. The standard lamp that had been knocked over produced a peculiar glow on that small portion of the front room ceiling visible from where we were.

I told Hamilton that one of us should take a brisk walk around the block, but he insisted we set to work immediately. So much for the man in the field always knowing best. So much for complaining about bodies being transported through the streets in wheelbarrows.

We both put on cotton gloves. When I got out of the van I could smell garlic and smoke.

I had made a point of not asking the minister for his keys to the house in Islington. This meant I had to scale the garden wall a second time. I did so, then I let in Hamilton with his bag and his cleaning things.

So, why remove the body at all? Why not just let them find it?

The answer is simple enough. A missing person doesn't get the attention a body gets. We were in the filing business. We were going to file Angela under Missing Persons. Permanently.

I chewed my lip while I picked the lock on the door at the back of the house. The door swung with a sigh on its hinges. Warm air hit me. That sweet aromatic smell filled my nostrils. I felt I had known that smell all my life.

Hamilton quietly closed the door behind him. We moved quickly up the stairs. Once we had made a preliminary inspection of each room Hamilton went back down the stairs. There was no bolt, no mortise lock on the door. He took two small wedges from his pocket. He jammed one between door and frame at the top, the other between the door and the wooden brace set in the floor. He then returned to the kitchen where I stood staring at Angela's body.

She had been lying on the floor for two hours now. Climbing the narrow staircase for a second time I had been filled with foreboding. I feared I would find her body in a different position. I would discover that she had survived the attack and that I could have saved her had I listened to her assailant when he demanded that we return to the scene.

But no. She lay as I had left her. There was more blood. Dark red blood. I couldn't take my eyes off her.

Hamilton acted like her killer. He glanced at her face once and thereafter merely treated her as something that belonged in his bag.

He laid the body bag out beside her and unzipped it. He caught her under her arms. I took her feet. We lifted her onto the bag. She was heavier than I had thought.

There was the smell of her perfume, the smell of plastic, the smell of feet. Would she turn her head or moan when Hamilton drew the zip over her face?

I looked at the shoe in the corner. Should I put it in the bag with her, should I put it on her foot, or, should I take the shoe she wore and put the pair in her bedroom? I felt I should do one of these things. I wasn't thinking about covering for the crime.

'Put it in,' Hamilton ordered. 'She's not starting a new life in her bare feet.'

I hadn't realized he was watching me. I picked up the stray shoe. I didn't toss it into the body bag. I put it on her foot. I felt ashamed.

Hamilton pulled over the flaps and drew the zip the length of her body. He began wiping the floor.

'Get packing,' he said.

I went into the bedroom to pack some of her things. I just couldn't believe I was doing this in light of the Lisa Talbot affair. The muscles in my neck were still locked. My arms seemed too short to reach the suitcase down from the wardrobe. My back ached when I bent to pull out the bottom drawer of a chest of drawers.

I needed a drink.

Most things she kept neatly folded. Where there was a jumble it was clear what belonged there. Everything had its place.

I was careful packing. I picked out a spare pair of shoes for her.

I was in the bathroom and Hamilton was on his hands and knees in the kitchen when we both heard the sound of a key being worked in the lock of the door at the bottom of the stairs.

The bedroom door and the kitchen door were nearest to the head of the stairs. I didn't want whoever it was entering the kitchen. I quickly took up position just inside the bedroom door. I took out my pistol. I would use the butt of it as a cosh.

Hamilton got up off his knees and came to the kitchen door. I signalled for him to move back, but when it became clear that his wedges were holding he moved to the head of the stairs and glared down at the door.

What was he doing? Tempting fate? Daring his handiwork to give way?

'Angela,' a man's voice shouted from the other side of the door. 'Angela, it's me – Alex. I can't open the door . . . Angie!'

He tried again. This time he attempted to force the door. 'Angela – come on, for God's sake!'

I looked at the black shape, Hamilton's body bag on the kitchen floor. It was filled to half capacity.

'Angela!' he shouted.

Judging by his impatient tone he had arrived in an agitated state. Now, he was angry.

Hamilton held his position at the head of the stairs. His face was glowing. I wasn't sure what I would do if the wedges gave way.

The caller tried the door a third time, then he pounded on the wooden panels with his fist.

'Open up, for God's sake. Let's talk.'

There was the sound of curtains being pulled back

sharply on a metal track. Then, the sound of sash weights operating. A muffled woman's voice from down below said: 'Will you *please* stop shouting.'

'Angela – I know you're in there,' the man's voice cried undeterred. 'Open the bloody door . . .'

'I'll not ask again,' said the woman in a firm, even voice. The window was then shut.

A moment later the door in the garden wall was slammed. Then, we heard the sound of a car door being slammed. Then, the sound of a car pulling away with a convulsive surge.

Hamilton returned to work without any communication.

It is strange to say, but I knew we would get away with carrying her body out of the house, through the garden, onto the street. I knew we would get her into the van without a hitch. It was as if we were doing the right thing.

'Who do you suppose that was?' I asked once we were on our way. 'Her boyfriend? Her ex-husband?'

'Boyfriend, I'd say,' Hamilton said with a smooth change of gear.

'Isn't anybody happy together?' I asked darkly. I was aching all over. I was jumpy. My small pistol seemed excessively heavy. It was cumbersome. It was causing me discomfort.

'My wife and I are happy,' Hamilton answered.

He meant it.

Hamilton and his wife were happy together.

Them, and my ex-wife with the bump on her nose and her new husband.

I thought about the cabinet minister rummaging in my papers. I thought about the way he stared at me, fixing my face in his memory. I think I counted the beads of sweat on his upper lip. I thought about Angela eating her lunch.

'This killing,' I said to Hamilton, 'does he get away with it?'

'We're not going to put him in gaol, if that is what you mean.'

'Is that what I mean?' I said indignantly, 'I don't know.'

There was a long pause. Hamilton seemed to be concentrating on his driving.

'You're going to tell me this whole thing has nothing to do with me, aren't you?' I ventured.

'My dear fellow,' he scoffed, 'I'm just helping you out. That's not to say you've done the wrong thing. On the contrary. It's certainly not something you've done for money because you won't be getting any extra.'

There was another silence between us, then Hamilton looked at me and grinned. 'Harry, are you after a desk job?'

There were more desk jobs, he told me. In this so-called new regime the emphasis had shifted, he explained. The fundamental question now was how intelligence was to be interpreted rather than how it was to be gathered. One got promoted and gained power by doing studies, he observed.

'Alas,' he said with a significant sigh, 'There is too much time invested in the theory of games. There are too many second-rate strategists undertaking studies in crowd behaviour.'

He was lecturing me again, pretending that he was being open and honest, that he was pointing the way for an ambitious operator like me. Hamilton's mockery springs from a deep place.

Hamilton drove to the cemetery in West Norwood. It's a large cemetery with a high wall. It has a crematorium.

He checked his watch as we travelled on the adjacent Robson Road. Perhaps he had made some arrangement before we met in Camden. He turned left and left again into the entrance bay. He got out of the van and unlocked the gate. It was the small hours. I counted three pedestrains at the junction who might have seen a blue transit van park at the cemetery gates. They might even have seen the van drive in through the gates. What of it? They might make a joke.

Hamilton didn't have to switch on the headlights to find his way once inside. He got us to the crematorium by the shortest route. He had a key to the crematorium, too.

It was so easy it was absurd. He had the keys. He knew how to operate the oven. It is not something you practise. He had done it before. Now it was my turn to pretend not to be shocked.

Before cremating Angela and her suitcase Hamilton said a prayer. He bowed his head before the body bag and spoke in a low, solemn voice. He commended the soul of this young woman to God.

I was strangely moved by this travesty. I wished I could have had faith enough to pray. As it was, I spoke her name and I mumbled 'Amen'.

People like Hamilton and me will be the last to survive on earth.

When it was done he meticulously gathered what was left. He took time to recover the small deposits of twisted and melted metals from the studs and buckles on the suitcase, from her watch, her rings, her fillings. I let him clean up. He seemed to like cleaning up.

We left the place as we had found it, save that for a time, it was warmer than it should have been. We two were the only people who would ever know where Angela had gone. As we drove away I felt this was a heavy burden.

Hamilton said he would ring me about the photographs. I would get my money when he had what he wanted. He was satisfied with the night's work. It was as if we had delivered a lion to the zoo.

I got out of the van at Vauxhall Bridge. There was still just twelve hundred miles on the clock.

I didn't want to go home. I wanted that drink. I pulled up my collar and I began to walk. I crossed the bridge at a slow pace. I looked into the river. It was low. The heavy clouds above just wouldn't let go. The wind whipped up litter on the pavement and sent it flying past me. I quickened my pace.

I had about a hundred and sixty pounds in my pocket. I walked all the way to Chinatown. I went to a place where you can drink and gamble till dawn. Cards mostly; sometimes dice or checkers; always sour whiskey out of a bottle you never see. A hundred and sixty quid doesn't go far in a place like that, but they know me there. I can get credit.

You don't see many women in this joint, but I saw my tall friend from the restaurant. She came in looking for somebody. She was upset. She saw me. I gave her one of my foolish grins. I know she recognized me by the way she let her eyes slide over me. I went looking for my friend Jimmy Mo. I wanted to ask him if he knew her, if he could tell me about her, if he could introduce us to each other. You get nowhere in Chinatown without an introduction.

Before I could find Jimmy she had left with two men. One of them was her brother-in-law. The other one must have been her husband. Whatever was upsetting her, it had to have been something serious. Her brother-in-law was on a winning streak.

By 5.00 a.m. I was drinking on credit with both hands. The smoke was getting thicker as the room got smaller. I swear, I could understand every word that was being uttered. I could hear somebody tell Jimmy Mo it was time he threw me out.

Jimmy let me stay. A couple of hours later he saw me onto the street. He made me promise to get a taxi home.

I bought a newspaper. I took the tube to Camden

Town. On the train I read about Lisa Talbot. She had been convicted of murder.

It took me a while to get out of the station. It seemed like a long walk to my car. I got in the car. I was drunk but I drove home. I just knew the police were not going to stop me.

The curtains remained shut in Lisa Talbot's flat. Perhaps the flat was already empty. Somebody else would be moving in.

I must have made a lot of noise parking the car. I must have revved the engine unnecessarily or scraped a hub-cap. The old woman who lives on the other side of me was looking out through a gap in her curtains when I was walking up the path. She never sleeps. She's a hardy woman with all her wits, but she gets things wrong. She thinks I'm unemployed because of the hours I keep. She thinks I feed her cat. I don't like cats.

I waved at her. She waved back.

Once inside, I took the film out of the camera and put it in my trouser pocket. I had no inclination to undress. I would be sleeping in my clothes.

The little red light on my answering machine was flashing. There were two messages. One was from Hamilton. He was wasting no time. He wanted to arrange a meeting. The other call was from Maureen Talbot. She wanted me to contact her. She gave me a number. She wouldn't say what it was about. Her sister had given her my number.

I was too drunk, too tired and too hungry to ring

anybody. I went to the kitchen before going to bed. Why do I look in the fridge when I know there is nothing in it to eat?

I laid my head on the pillow. I closed my eyes. It began to pour.

CHAPTER 4

WATCH HARRY DIG

The rain had washed Angela out of the sky and down the drains. There was a fresh damp breeze that whistled through a tiny gap in the window frame of my living room. These are one-bedroom flats with a spare boxroom. They were built in 1959. They accommodate single pensioners, widows, divorcees and misfits like myself. Many of the residents fall into more than one of these categories. Many of the windows whistle in the wind. None of us is inclined to do anything about it.

The tiny gap in my window frame sang a demon lullaby, but I slept all day. It was dark when I woke. I saw the moon rise out of a slit in the ground. Behind me the red light on my answering machine was flashing in the dark. Hamilton had rung three times during the day.

I use the boxroom as a walk-in suitcase and make-shift darkroom. I have installed blackout blinds. I have hung heavy velvet curtains I bought second-hand. They used to hang across the porthole doors in a cinema. The boxroom is on the corner. It has two small windows, one facing south, the other east. It's my one-storey tower. I sit in there sometimes on a fold-up chair. I thought Hamilton might be sitting outside in one of his cars so I got my binoculars from the desk drawer and I went into the boxroom without switching on the light. The curtains were open and the blinds were raised. I stood well back and scanned the parked vehicles on both streets. If Hamilton was out there I couldn't see him.

I went to the kitchen to make myself a pot of coffee. I found Hamilton sitting on one of the two chairs, his coat buttoned, his shining shoes placed snugly together.

'You snore, do you know that?' he said.

I smiled at him tenderly, then I kicked the chair he was sitting on and it collapsed.

'Be careful,' I said as he reached to pull himself off the floor, 'that's got a wonky leg.'

Today, Hamilton was a smug bastard. He wanted to show me that he was as good if not better than me at my job. He should have asked if he could sit down. I would have offered him the safe chair.

The fall had ruffled his feathers. When he got to his feet he came straight to the point. He asked for the negatives and prints. He slapped an envelope with money in it on the table. I picked it up, ripped it open, made a point of counting the bank notes. Then, I told him he would have to wait.

I would have what he wanted by twelve o'clock, I told him. He could wait outside in his car, or, he could go home and cook dinner for his wife and children.

He said nothing. He walked out. He left the door open.

I wanted breakfast. It was almost eleven o'clock at night. What of it? Some people go fishing at night.

I ate a fry-up in a local cafeteria. As I ate I was thinking I would go for a drink in some late-night kip. I would need something to sit on this food in my stomach while I thought hard about my lousy life. I had some decisions to make.

The cafeteria was busy, but orders were moving slowly. I felt a little better sitting here. I need to be among people if I am to avoid being self-destructive. When I am among strangers the contradictions that plague me make sense. I am reminded that every day ordinary people privately undertake extraordinary acts of kindness and bravery.

What was my situation? I had witnessed a second killing. This time I had photographs of a cabinet minister stabbing his mistress with a steak knife.

I no longer revelled in the power of my secret for I had felt compelled to share that secret with Hamilton, the queen's messenger, the grand master and invisible politician, the arch deceiver. This time I had helped dispose of the body. This time I was sickened enough to want to pray.

I had done my job, and more besides. Hamilton had committed himself to protecting this man for whatever gain, whatever triumph he saw on the horizon. Hamilton thrived on mistrust and the fear it bred. No show of loyalty would extricate me from the danger I was now exposed to. If he wanted to get rid of me it would be easy enough provided he or any crew of thugs he cared to assemble could find me.

Should I go to ground? Should I confront Hamilton? I could arrange to have a bundle of photographs sent to the newspapers if I were to disappear or if an unfortunate accident were to cause my death. Believe me, there is no satisfaction to be had from such a scheme. It guarantees nothing. Take that from somebody whose job entails, among other activities, breaking and entering.

While I was worrying about staying alive my elderly neighbour was standing outside on the pavement waving at me through the plate glass window. Eventually, I looked up and saw her. It was a bold but not unfriendly wave. If I had disturbed her the previous night she had forgiven me.

I returned her wave. She took this as an invitation. She came in.

'Murder,' she said in a loud voice, as she sat down opposite me in the booth. 'It isn't right, is it? Did you read the papers? I don't know what it is but it isn't murder. Her sister, it seems, was too timid to stand up to him. Add up all the beatings her sister has suffered. It amounts to provocation. Cumulative provocation.'

She ordered a cup of tea.

'She shouldn't have buried him, though. She should have brought what was left of the brute to the police station. She would have got off with manslaughter. There's women who get beaten and raped all their married lives – longer than any sentence for manslaughter . . .'

For all her misjudgement, here was something she had got right.

The tea arrived. It was hotter than a finger could tolerate, but she took a mouthful directly. She liked it that way.

'Did I disturb you last night, Missus Lamb?' I asked 'If I did I'm sorry.'

'You didn't disturb me,' she said. 'I thought you might be another one of those newspaper photographers. I don't know how many times they've photographed the building. What do they hope to capture? It's only a pile of bricks. The curtains in her flat are closed.'

She looked at what was left on my plate. Curiosity gave way to disgust.

'I'd say they have all the pictures they want by now, Missus Lamb,' I said.

She leaned forward slightly and, dropping her voice said: 'I think they want inside.' She pulled in her chin. She tightened her lips. 'They want photographs of the furniture. They want to go through her things. They want her family photographs so they can print them in their newspapers.'

She drank more tea. She withdrew for a moment.

'I was lucky,' she said. 'Bill was a good man. Look at him,' she scoffed, as if I could see her dead husband out on the pavement, 'a man without an ounce of romance in him, born on Saint Valentine's Day.'

She finished her tea. She drinks a lot of tea. She ordered a second cup.

'I've had the one man,' she said. 'I've never wanted

another. That young woman's sister – she's the sort that deserves a second chance, wouldn't you say . . . ?' She wouldn't refer to Lisa Talbot by name.

'Yes . . . you're right,' I mumbled.

'Do you think they planned it together?' she asked abruptly. 'To kill him, I mean . . .'

It looked as if she had been carrying the newspaper with her all day. She had it rolled tightly in her coat pocket. She pulled it out now and spread it on the table, as Hamilton had done. She smoothed it with the heel of her palm. She turned to the article on Lisa Talbot. She studied the press photographs intently.

'You don't seem to care much for her plight, Mister Fielding,' she said without looking up.

I assured her of my concern. I lamely excused my silence by telling her that I had not yet recovered from the shock of our neighbour having been convicted of murder.

I insisted that her teas be put on my bill. Then, I found I hadn't enough small change. I had to pay with a fifty-pound note out of the envelope Hamilton had given me.

I didn't go for a drink. Instead, I walked the old woman to her door. In the entrance hall to our building what I had come to identify as widows' perfume had been replaced by the smell of Angela's perfume. It was my imagination, of course. I had a lot on my mind.

I had a drink in the boxroom before I set to work developing and printing. I decided that I had been over-reacting. The Lisa Talbot affair and the grisly events of the previous night had combined to create in me an irrational fear. I would finish the job. I would keep my back to the wall. I would be ready to go to ground. Hamilton would assume I had made a second set of prints regardless. There was nothing I could do about that.

Hamilton changed his mind about giving me something extra. He brought a half bottle of whiskey when he returned promptly at twelve o'clock. It was the cheapest half bottle he could find. He put it on the kitchen table without saying anything. I offered him a chair but he wouldn't sit down. He said he was in a hurry.

One set of prints were drying. I had them strung up in the boxroom. Hamilton pretended he wasn't interested in their content. He had just come to collect them. The queen's messenger is always in a hurry.

I put the prints in an envelope. I gave him the unbroken roll of negatives. I moved my stiff shoulders. My face went blank.

'That's it, then,' I said.

'For now,' he replied. 'You *have* done well,' he said pausing in the doorway. Clearly, he thought I needed reassurance.

I thought by the way he cast a cold eye over my living room that he was going to offer to clean it out.

'We will all benefit from this,' he added, turning back to me.

My face remained blank while I tried to read what was in his eyes. I gave a sharp nod in the direction of the kitchen table. 'I've done well out of it already,' I said.

My ungratefulness didn't bother him. He gave a weak grin.

'I'll be in touch.'

'I'm sure you will,' I said.

I rang Maureen Talbot the following morning. The number she had left on my answering machine was her home number. She hadn't gone to work. The press had laid siege to her house. She wanted my help. Lisa had given her my number because I had told her that I worked as a picture researcher. She naively assumed that such a person might have some influence with press reporters and editors. I was the only 'media person' she knew. She thought I might be able to arrange for Maureen to make one brief statement and thereafter be left in peace.

They were camped outside Maureen's door in Wandsworth. They probably had a tap on her telephone line.

I told Maureen I would call to her at 10.30 that morning. I took a taxi to Wandsworth. It was 9.30 when I got out two streets away from where she lived. I sent the driver on with a note. Twenty minutes later he returned with Maureen in the taxi and the press posse following behind. I got into the taxi and we drove to Balham tube station. We hurried down into the tunnel. One photographer and one reporter caught up with us. They called to Maureen, using her first name as if they were spurned lovers looking for forgiveness. A train entered the station just as they closed on us. I took Maureen by the arm. We got into one carriage. I made sure we stood by the doors. They got in the same carriage by the door at the end. I waited a moment then, as they advanced, I abruptly stepped back onto the platform, taking Maureen with me. I led her further up the platform. They got back out by the door through which they had entered, but they were reluctant to follow. They knew what I was at. The photographer took several pictures from where he stood. His companion attempted to negotiate an interview. His voice got louder as we got further away. 'Who are you, sir?' he called out when he got no reply. 'Who is he, Maureen?'

I glanced back, past them, to the guard in the last carriage. Our friends knew we were going to jump into the nearest carriage just before the doors closed. We did just that, though I had to push Maureen forcefully. I didn't want her anticipating the move as they did. I timed the move well. For all their readiness, they missed their chance. They should have gone to the middle of the carriage where there were double doors. They wouldn't have crowded each other. Only one of them managed to get on. The reporter. I got us off at the next station just before the the doors closed. He wasn't quick enough to follow. We caught the next train.

Maureen was upset and angry at my having pushed

her onto the train. She had been bullied and frightened enough. I should have told her what I had planned, she said. She wasn't slow. Nor was she stupid.

I apologized. Only then did I realize I was still clutching her arm. I let go immediately.

We changed at Leicester Square. We got out at Hyde Park Corner. I took her rowing on the Serpentine.

All this dodging and pushing and there was nothing I could do to protect her. If they hadn't already tapped her telephone line they would be tapping it now while she was out of the house. She had caught them rummaging in her dustbin, she told me. They had rented the living room of her neighbour's house across the street to accommodate photographers with telephoto lenses.

She had been utterly unprepared for all this. She had drawn the curtains at the front of the house. She had not thought to do the same at the back.

The tabloids were calling the killing of Frank Morley a tragedy, but there was the veiled suggestion that the whole story had yet to be revealed in their pages. Maureen Talbot, a victim of domestic violence, was getting a new start in life. She was benefiting from a murder committed in her name. Could she be entirely innocent? Did she *really* know nothing of the killing prior to the discovery of her husband's body in a shallow grave in the woods? WIFE DENIES INVOLVEMENT. What kind of sisters were these?

The killing was being portrayed as an act of

revenge, not an act of defence. This lent more weight to the conspiracy theory. If Maureen Talbot were to admit that she had a part in it she could tell her story in their pages and the nation would forgive her.

As I rowed she told me how frightened she was and asked if there was anything I could do to help her.

I lied. I told her I would call somebody I knew at the Press Complaints Commission. She swallowed that. I advised her that she should leave regardless. She should stay the night with friends. She should then get out of the country, for a time at least.

The relief showed on her face. That was what she wanted to do. She had been waiting for somebody to tell her to leave. She could not leave Lisa in gaol and run entirely of her own accord.

I offered her money in case she had need of it, but she declined. She wanted to apologize for having to ask a stranger for help. Her friends were as frightened as she was, she explained, though perhaps for different reasons.

She said she would delay her departure only to visit Lisa. I said that I would accompany her if she wished. This offer she gladly accepted. She then asked if I wanted her to row. She said that she could make a better job of it than I.

There were press photographers and reporters at the entrance to Holloway. They had been informed by one of the screws. Maureen set an even pace from the car to the gate. She wouldn't have wanted me to take her arm. In any case, she cleared a path through them better than I could have.

Lisa was allowed to embrace her sister. They held each other tightly and rocked. Lisa was first to let go. She needed to show that she had lost none of her resolve.

She was managing to ignore the screw standing by the door. She made us sit down. She was in good spirits, she told us. She had been getting messages of support from strangers, she said. She was determined to fight her case through the appeal courts. She told us she slept without having nightmares. She had no regrets save the trouble she had brought Maureen. Could Maureen forgive her for the thing she had done?

Lisa was not sorry for what she had done but there was a sadness in her that was not a healing sadness.

She gave a tight smile. Maureen burst into tears. She cried for all the suffering she herself had foolishly endured and for the trouble she had brought her sister.

Maureen is going to leave for a while, I told Lisa. Lisa readily approved. She made her sister promise to write daily. Was she returning to Ireland? No. Maureen was going to stay with friends in Amsterdam, for a fortnight to begin with.

Maureen told her she had talked to their mother on the telephone. Lisa cut her short. She didn't want to know any more than that. The old woman could never understand.

She knew I would be accompanying Maureen

to the prison. Maureen had told her as much. However, Lisa had acted surprised when I stepped into the room. She kept looking at me now. I could see she was desperately afraid. I could see she was panicking. I could do nothing.

She was not to worry about Maureen, I told her. Maureen had everything in hand I assured her, as if Maureen was in another place. Maureen was sitting close beside me on one of the three hard chairs. The hollow assurance I offered her sister had the effect of one of Lisa's supportive strangers sitting down between us.

Lisa kept her eyes on me. She was able to see that now I could only love a woman who would do what she had done. I should have kept my eyes shut.

Hamilton rang me. He had seen a photograph of me escorting Maureen Talbot into Holloway prison in one of the newspapers. What the hell did I think I was doing? Did I not realize how substantial a service he had performed clearing me of any involvement in the Talbot case? Was I trying to make a fool of him?

I told him I had just seen our cabinet minister with the Prime Minister on the six o'clock news. Fit him better to ponder that.

He didn't like my remark. It was unprofessional. Worse than that, it was in bad taste.

The days that followed had no shape. I'm used to days like that. I don't fret. I get out in the streets. I visit some old haunts. I go abroad on my own time. I'm on holiday, I tell myself when I look in my pockets. That's why I have a little extra to spend.

I see gangsters in late afternoon pull up in their cars to check on their investments. They are just out of bed. I see plain-clothes coppers pull up in their cars to check their investments. They've got out of bed at seven in the morning. Whether these people want information or they want to shake the money tree, they go in pairs.

I despised Hamilton, but he and I were a pair. I asked myself what was the difference between us? Background, rank, influence. What would he do that I would not do? I feared that in this respect there was no difference at all. I could see myself getting a key to the lock-up in Spitalfields.

I didn't want to work for Hamilton any more. I wanted to be inside, to be part of the family. I had never in my life felt safe. I wanted to feel safe. I wanted Hamilton's chair at the club.

Part 2

NOT LEVEL

CHAPTER 5

THE SHADOW BOX

I keep a billiard-ball in the bathroom. I don't play billiards. It's not a keepsake. It doesn't remind me of anybody. I found it in the gutter one night so I brought it home. It was so smooth and clean it seemed to belong in the bathroom. I found a use for it. I knock on the bathroom wall with it just to let Missus Lamb know I'm thinking about her. She lives on her own. She doesn't have visitors. She has never passed comment on my knocking, though she knocks in response. She will also knock in the evening if she has seen somebody call to my door while I'm out. I can hear her knock from anywhere in my flat. Maybe she has found a billiard-ball in the gutter. A billiard-ball gives a nice clean note on a dividing wall.

I was staring at that billiard-ball in the soap dish. I had one leg dangling heavily over the rim of the bath. I had let the water run out. I was thinking I might stay there for a week or more just blinking my eyelids. I had left the television on in the living room. When I heard Angela Richardson's name mentioned I sprang out of that bath tub so damn quickly I nearly slipped and broke my neck.

It was strange and unsettling to see Alex Simson on the television taking part in a reconstruction of Angela Richardson's last known movements. Angela had been formally listed as a missing person. The police had evidently decided that her disappearance was not voluntary. They were convinced that she had been abducted, though they were not saying it outright. There had been a series of abductions that ended in murder in the capital of late. There was strong circumstantial evidence to suggest that a number of these cases were the work of one killer. His victims were female, in their late twenties or early thirties. Apart from that, he seemingly struck at random. There was no social, racial or neigh-bourhood link. The reports in the newspapers had been scant. There had been no arrest. There was no prime suspect. There would be those who would tirelessly search for some small link between Angela Richardson's disappearance and the circumstances under which this killer's victims had vanished.

Alex Simson looked older than I had imagined when Hamilton and I stood by the body of his girlfriend and let him pound on her door. His build was slight. I had an image of a tall heavy-set man.

It had been less than a month since Angela had vanished. I had assumed that within three months hers would be a cold case. This item on the crime programme altered my expectations. The police investigation would be prolonged. What was their line of enquiry? I watched carefully, naked in my chair.

The policewoman playing the part of Angela Richardson didn't look at all like her. Though they had got the clothing right, her hair was wrong. So, too, were her shoes. The woman who served Angela from behind the counter at the delicatessen had remembered her coming in late for lunch. In the reconstruction she put her sitting at the wrong table. Angela had spent the previous night in Alex Simson's flat in Fulham. He had telephoned her at the cutting rooms in the West End late the following morning to say that he would not be able to meet her for lunch as planned. He had called at her flat in Islington late that night – at about twelve o'clock, he said. This was confirmed by Angela Richardson's downstairs neighbour. In fact, Alex Simson had come pounding on his girlfriend's door some three-quarters of an hour later than he had stated.

The police would have asked the staff of the delicatessen for a description of other customers who had entered the premises that afternoon. They would have been particularly interested in single men. The police were anxious to have anybody who was in the delicatessen between the hours of twelve noon and four o'clock that afternoon contact them.

The woman who had served Angela Richardson stated that Angela had eaten her lunch in a hurry and had left the delicatessen alone.

That was the last known sighting of Angela Richardson, we were told. Had she met somebody on the short journey from the delicatessen to the cutting rooms where she worked? Had she set off for another destination? The police wanted to hear from anybody who might have seen her on the street.

The old man in Angela's local grocery shop had probably recognized her when he was shown a photograph, but presumably had not remembered her coming into his shop on that particular day. The police would have searched the kitchen rubbish bin in Angela's flat and perhaps found a dated receipt from that shop in the corner of a plastic carrier bag that showed she or somebody visiting her must have purchased goods in his shop. This in itself told the detectives relatively little. The old man could not remember somebody purchasing this particular selection of groceries. However, they would have noted that some of the items purchased had been used in preparing dinner for two.

Had Alex told the police they had had a row after all? That was the impression I was getting as I watched him now invite the public to assist the police in their search.

The reconstruction had shown him knocking on her door – about the same pitch I achieve knocking on Missus Lamb's wall with the billiard-ball. It had shown Angela's downstairs neighbour raising her window to complain about the noise he was making. Alex Simson was not faring well under the pressure of close scrutiny.

I got up and went into the bedroom. I put on a vest, then I sat on the bed. If I got back into bed I would wake with the sheet bunched between my teeth. I had been sleeping too much of late and it wasn't doing me any good. I was waking with the shivers. I put on my clothes and went for a long walk.

I avoid the park. Birdsong distracts me. Animals make me nervous. Animals and madmen. I was once so anxious to cross the street to avoid a madman approaching from behind that I stepped out in front of a car. I was lucky. I got away with a sprained ankle and some nasty bruising. The madman stood on the kerb shouting abuse at the driver. I wear a vest all year round for fear of catching a cold, but I don't always look when I'm crossing the street.

I thought about Angela Richardson's killing. A succession of stark and disturbing images paraded themselves before me. I pieced together in my mind sufficient circumstantial detail to allow me to prowl her flat retrospectively, to search it for clues as the police would have done. I retraced each step Hamilton and I had taken. In doing this I walked with my head pitched forward. To anybody who passed me on the pavement I must have given the impression of a lost soul with too much humility.

I didn't fret. I just knew we three were going to get away with it. It's the Lisa Talbots of this world who get caught.

I kept walking until it began to rain. Then I went to an hotel bar I frequent where it rained in my glass for the rest of the evening.

*   *   *

I took a taxi back to my flat. Missus Lamb greeted me in the passageway in her dressing gown.

'There's somebody in there,' she said in a quiet voice, indicating my door. 'A man. I didn't want to ring the police. I thought he might be a friend of yours. Let himself in, he did.'

I didn't respond immediately. She looked at me severely.

'I'll ring the police if you like,' she said speculatively.

I wasn't drunk, just a little slow.

'What does he look like?' I asked. If it was Hamilton again I was going to bounce him out of there.

'Black,' she said flatly. 'A handsome boy. He's dressed in one of those nylon catsuits they wear.'

'Ah – that's . . . alright. That'll be Lee . . . Has he been here long?'

'Twenty minutes,' she said, 'I've had the clock on him.'

'I thought I'd be back earlier,' I mumbled.

There was another short silence while I decided what to do. Missus Lamb's severe look was supplemented by a show of impatience. 'I don't mind, you know,' she said firmly. 'You can have whoever you like round here. *I* don't care.'

'Thank you, Missus Lamb.'

I wanted her back inside her own flat before I made a move. I took my time rooting for my key.

'Anyway,' she said somewhat vaguely, '*I* don't think the birds and bees know the difference . . .'

I grinned stupidly at her. I was swaying a little on my feet. I would be alright once I moved.

She focused again. 'It's just we all have to be careful,' she said significantly. She finally realized that I wanted her to withdraw. 'Anyway,' she said dully, 'he's in there . . .'

'Thanks,' I said.

I didn't make a sound opening the door. I took my time. When I emerged from the short passageway into the living room he had his back to me. He was bent over, looking down behind the desk which he had pulled out from the wall.

No doubt you have thought about it at one time or another – you hear a noise in the middle of the night – you have to decide whether or not you should go downstairs. Are you really prepared to confront a burglar? Frankly, this scenario is not a problem for me. I know how they work. I do the job myself. I know what they fear. I just have to decide whether or not I'm going to beat him until his head is as big as a dustbin.

When my friend came to he found himself tied to my kitchen chair, the one with the good legs. I'd had a good look around to see what he had taken. He was tidy, I'll say that for him. Scarcely a thing out of place. No doubt he would have pushed the desk back against the wall had I not disturbed him. He had a black canvas bag with a drawstring. It had some of my things in it. Camera gear mostly. There was also a broken gold watch I had inherited but had not bothered to get fixed, a silver-plated pen, and a roll of bank notes I keep for small emergencies or for the rare nights I'm feeling lucky.

I had been through his pockets. He had brought nothing that would identify him. He had some thirty pounds cash, car keys, two keys for a hall door. He carried a fancy set of lock-picks. He wore an expensive pair of trainers. There were no needle marks on his limbs.

He groaned and let out a nauseous whine. His eyes focused on me momentarily, then on the picture cord that bound him.

'What have you done?' he asked painfully.

'I've waited patiently,' I replied.

'You hit me . . . you . . .'

'Oh, I did,' I confirmed.

'What did you hit me with?' he demanded with the same pain evident in his voice.

'With conviction,' I said assuredly. 'What's your name?' I asked.

He wasn't going to tell me.

'A first name will do.'

He had a tic in one eye that made me want to slap his face.

'Winston. I'll call you Winston.'

No response.

'Winston,' I said, 'these days there's a lack of social cohesion that makes it increasingly difficult for us all to decide what we mean to each other . . . wouldn't you agree?'

He sneered. I slapped his face hard. He agreed there was a lack of social cohesion.

'I mean, it's difficult for me to know what I should do with you. I don't know where you belong. I just know you don't belong here. Are you a charity case? I ask myself. How do you feel about charity, Winston? Do you think people give enough?'

Winston sat there with his mouth firmly shut, and still, a little blood managed to get out.

'I get upset when I go into a charity shop. They're going to give people a better life with this lot, I say to myself, then I feel desperately ashamed. I want to buy everything in the shop. Do you ever feel like that, Winston, when you're robbing some old woman's flat?'

Alright, so I *was* a little drunk.

Winston shook his head. No. He had never felt like that. Not ever.

'You picked the wrong flat, pal,' I told him. There was an old woman living on her own next door, I advised him. Never gets a visit. Has to go out for her sliced pan. The person on the other side of me was away on holidays, I told him. She had a good job.

I went out of the kitchen. I got my camera from his bag. I put on the lens I wanted. I loaded a fresh roll of film. I went back into the kitchen.

'I know what you do for a living,' I said. 'Now, me,' I said, 'I'm a copper who likes to take photographs.'

I kicked the chair back on two legs. He cracked his sore head on the kitchen counter, thereby preventing the chair from toppling completely. I took Winston's photograph.

I thought he was going to be sick. He made another unpleasant noise. I untied him. He was giddy from both blows. Also, I think I had tied the cord too tightly. I kicked him in the arse. I told him that if he came within a mile of this place again I'd have my pals caution him in the back of a moving van.

He was young and cocky but I had him a little scared. He could hardly stand up. I think he was concussed. I made him empty the rest of the items out of his bag in the living room. I pointed to the expensive watch he wore on his wrist.

'Nice watch,' I said. 'Is it yours? Of course it's yours. You stole it.'

I took it from him. I gave him the broken family heirloom in lieu.

'That's yours now,' I said and I kicked him in the arse again. Then I bounced him out of my flat.

I didn't want another drink. I didn't want to gamble. I didn't want to eat or sleep. I could go for another long walk, I thought. My ex-wife lives a mile and a half up the road. I could take a walk over there and see how normal people live. She had married her boyfriend after I had battered his car with the club. Perhaps my doing the job on his car precipitated the move. Couples who survive accidents or other such traumatic events often marry or split up as a result. This man was really proud of his car.

I got back into the bath.

It was 3.00 a.m. It was quiet out on the streets.

I could hear the wind in the window frames. I wondered if our man was lying awake in the dark beside his sleeping wife. Could he smell Angela's perfume? I could smell it now. Maybe Alex Simson had bought her another bottle of the stuff to make up with her.

I thought about the steak knives slowly sinking in the mud at the bottom of the river. My bath water went cold. I pulled the plug and let it run out. I lay there motionless, blinking occasionally. Then, I heard noises coming from Lisa Talbot's flat. The twittering of furniture wheels.

I got out of the damn bath as quickly as before. I pulled on some clothes and went outside. The curtains remained closed at the front but the interior of Lisa Talbot's flat was lit. I went around to the back. The kitchen blind was raised. I could see through to the living room. Maureen Talbot was pushing furniture into one corner of the room to make way for cardboard boxes. She was packing the remaining items belonging to her sister into the boxes. Her approach lacked method but she worked fast.

I stood and watched for a considerable time while she moved about the flat. I stood close to the window. I didn't try to hide myself. When eventually she saw me she jumped with fright. I didn't intend to scare her. I wanted her to see me. I wanted to return the penetrating look she had given me in the rowing boat, a look I did not fully understand.

She opened the door to me. She had already recovered from her fright.

'What are you doing here?' she asked in a hushed voice. 'Did I disturb you?'

'I thought you were in Amsterdam,' I said.

'I'm going,' she said looking behind me into the street as though she was expecting trouble. 'I just need to take away Lisa's things. The landlord will throw her things out into the street if I don't take them.'

She was packing her sister's belongings in the middle of the night because she did not want the press people watching. The Talbot case would quickly vanish from the pages of the tabloids but Maureen would suffer from the exposure for a very long time to come.

I offered to help her pack. She said I could help her lift the boxes. She didn't want me packing.

Where was she going to put the stuff? I asked. She had no car. How was she going to transport it? Had she somebody waiting with a car? What about the furniture?

She was going to sell the furniture and have the buyer collect it. She was going to take the rest by taxi to her house in Wandsworth. She would store it there, though she would soon be getting out of that house.

I told her she could store some of it in my boxroom. She readily accepted my offer.

Missus Lamb came out of her flat when she heard us carting the boxes out of one flat into the other. When I tried to introduce Maureen she scoffed.

'I know who she is,' she said. She was at pains to

stress that she recognized Maureen from her visits to her sister rather than from seeing her photograph in the newspapers. 'I'm sorry, love,' she said good-naturedly to Maureen, 'things must be difficult enough without having to do this sort of thing with him for help.' She offered to take whatever I could not fit in my room. She offered to make tea.

I told her we'd be having tea later.

'Suit yourselves,' she said, '*I* don't care.'

I told her I would transfer whatever I could not store into her flat the following day.

Lisa Talbot's boxes would be safe with her, she assured Maureen.

'We should have let her make the tea,' Maureen said when the old woman had shut her door.

'*I'll* make you tea,' I insisted, 'right now.'

She didn't want tea. I found that out in the kitchen when I offered her the one good chair. Instead of sitting she embraced me. She kept her eyes open. I felt my arms move to close around her. I had not instructed them to do such a thing.

'You should be in Amsterdam with your friends,' I said.

I began to rock her gently. Self-consciously I tried to do it as Lisa had done it. Maureen tightened her grip.

She stayed that night. She got into my unmade bed with me. I blundered through the remaining hours of darkness making love clumsily. She tried to match my clumsiness. It was a kind of passion I had never before encountered.

In the morning I again told her to go to her friends in Amsterdam. She assured me that she was going, then she got dressed and went to buy milk for the coffee. She returned so quickly she must have run to and from the shop.

I didn't get to move any of Lisa Talbot's belongings into Missus Lamb's flat that day. I got a call from Hamilton. He wanted to see me urgently. That suited me. I had something I wanted to see him about.

He was sitting outside in his car. I was to come out. I let him wait. I took a look at him through my binoculars. The print of Winston was still wet but I unpegged it. I put on my jacket. I considered taking the Beretta. I decided to leave it. I went out and got into Hamilton's car. He didn't say a word. He turned the key in the ignition and we took off down the street.

I thought if he wasn't going to speak I would say my piece. I took the print of Winston from my pocket. It was still damp. I slapped it onto the windscreen in front of me and it stuck.

'Never mind making it look like a burglary,' I said, 'you should have just given him a set of your wedges and let him at it. His first job, is it?'

Hamilton didn't so much as flinch. He glanced at the photograph of Winston tied to the chair. He switched on the air blower for the windscreen. He was driving an old Humber today. The fan in the dashboard of a Humber gives a good blast of air. The photograph promptly lifted off the windscreen.

'I can't imagine what you thought he might find,' I said.

Hamilton remained silent. Just to show I had a mature grasp of the situation generally I let that be my concluding remark on Winston. I picked the photograph off the floor of the car and I put it in Hamilton's glove compartment.

'You saw Alex Simson on television?' I asked presently. For the first time since I had got into the car Hamilton spoke.

'If I want entertainment I go to the opera,' he said in the most even and chilling of Whitehall voices. He knew what I was referring to. Most likely Alex Simson's name would have presented itself early in Hamilton's investigation of our man's affair with Angela Richardson. He would have been updated by those who could not be aware of the fatal encounter.

I cultivated the silence that followed, then I said, 'I expect a great many people who saw that programme are thinking Angela Richardson isn't missing, she's dead. They're thinking Angela is dead and her boyfriend, Alex Simson, the man we've just seen on our telly, strangled her.' I left a little pause then I turned to Hamilton blankly and said, 'Who knows, maybe they're right.'

I knew by the aggressive way Hamilton was driving it would be pointless for me to ask where we were going. We were heading east, into dock-lands, so I knew we weren't going for breakfast at the Ritz. We weren't going to our favourite motorway cafeteria either. I didn't fret – but I should have.

Hamilton stopped the car in a laneway. The door on my side was opened. I felt a sharp stab in my arm. It seemed to take a long time to turn my head. A hulk of a man in shirt sleeves and braces was leaning in on top of me. His eyes were bulging. They were set to burst out of his head. There was another man. He was standing back from the car. Small. Bald. Grinning. I saw him through the windscreen. He was standing to attention on bandy legs. Maybe it wasn't a grin. Maybe he had a permanent frown from spending too much time picking at his teeth.

Chaps. I was sure of it.

'That'll do nicely, George,' I heard Hamilton say drily to the big man.

My head became impossibly heavy. It fell forwards. The last I saw of my assailants was the small bald one advancing like a wading marsh bird. The closer he got the more his eyes bulged, the wider his spurious grin grew.

I tumbled. My heels rose up behind me and passed effortlessly through the roof of the car before my forehead hit the dashboard. The dashboard gave way. I acted surprised though I was not at all surprised that it split asunder. Anybody can act surprised.

I kept on tumbling until I was able to reach for the Beretta I hadn't brought. Here was another of those surprises. The gun was right where I hadn't put it. When I pulled it out I was on my back. I fired. It spat diamonds. I made small holes in the roof of Hamilton's car. For a moment, the light shone through. The little holes were like stars. Then, everything went black and I felt sick. Hamilton's words echoed in my ears – 'That'll do nicely, George.' I tried to whistle to drown them out.

I was still trying to whistle when I regained consciousness. I was still on my back. I was still in the dark. The only light came from the crack under the door. I could reach down and touch the bare wooden floor. I was lying on a soldier's cot. I could reach down to the floor. I could turn my head slowly. That was as much as I could do. They didn't need to tie my hands and feet. I had been pumped full of drugs. I couldn't have got off that cot to save my life. I told you that I could reach down and touch the floor. I didn't say I could get my arm back up on the cot.

The light from under the door was intense to my eyes, but it scarcely reached into the room. I could not look at it for any length of time. I would only look in that direction when I heard the footsteps. When there were no footsteps there was an artificial silence. I had decided I was in a room within a room. Though I could not judge the dimensions of this room by sight, I sensed it was small from the tentative noises I permitted myself to make. I thought I might be able to surface under my own steam whilst pretending to remain deep in the dark hole in which I had been put.

Who was I trying to fool?

The footsteps came at irregular intervals. I tried

hard to concentrate. If I could just keep track for a few consecutive seconds.

Which way was out? I had established that there was a corridor on the other side of the door. It ran at right angles to my room. My gaoler entered from the right, or was it the left? How many paces to that other heavy door I had heard open and close? I hadn't been able to concentrate long enough to count.

When the outer door closed I could hear no more footfalls. I was left with that artificial silence, and the sound of my own breathing.

Was my visitor always the same person? Did I hear the same rhythm in the footsteps? What could I tell by their sound? Military bearing or not? Big man or small?

When the door opened I kept my eyes shut and practised shallow breathing. It wasn't difficult. I desperately wanted to sleep. I wanted to tumble into oblivion. I had to fight to stay conscious. Staying conscious was the most difficult task I had ever undertaken.

It might have been Hamilton who visited me. Whoever it was they stayed a long time. I sensed that they sat patiently in the dark, watching me.

How long had I been in this room? Hours? Weeks? A month? The place smelt of cat piss, sulphur and expensive cigars, but I had not heard or sensed the presence of a cat, nor had I heard the puffing or seen the glow from a lighted cigar, nor heard the scratching or seen the burst of light from a match.

The inevitable happened. Somebody switched on

the light. That was after they had filled me with more junk. I started seeing things in such detail it was frightening. That state alternated with a terrifying blindness – I was seeing through a dead man's eyes. As a measure of how confused I was in my mind let me tell you that I thought I was Frank Morley clawing his way out of the dirt with the car headlights burning the eyes out of his head.

Whether or not Hamilton had been my visitor in the dark, he was there to greet me when the light came on. He wasn't impressed with anything I was saying. If it had been him patiently watching me in the dark, he had lost his patience.

He put me sitting on a hard chair at a small table in the middle of the room. I had to grip the table-top at either end to keep from falling over. He showed me a bunch of photographs of our cabinet minister with Angela Richardson. All the time he was shouting at me. I didn't know what he was saying. I just knew it was important that he grasped that they weren't my photographs. I told him as much, but he didn't listen. When he had worked his way through the bundle, snapping one photograph down onto another, he would start again. I kept telling him they weren't my photographs. I kept talking until I tumbled backwards into the darkness and the silence.

CHAPTER 6

HARRY IN THE RAIN

Alex Simson was a journalist. The scoop that was to afford him the reputation he deserved was a long time in coming, and now that the story had burst in his lap it had gone sour. Alex was prepared to resort to dirty tricks so that later he might demonstrate his powers of insight whilst being seen to exercise discretion. In that respect we were alike.

The photographs Hamilton had repeatedly slapped on the table in front of me in the sweat room were Alex Simson's work. Simson had learnt of the affair between his girlfriend, Angela, and our man, the cabinet minister, before Hamilton knew of it. Our man had received that same bundle of photographs through the post at his home address. There was no message enclosed. This delivery was just to open with.

Career aside, Alex Simson was an angry man, a jilted lover. Evidently, he was an opportunist who fancied he had a talent for blackmail. Our man had rung Hamilton immediately.

'I have some bad news,' he had told Hamilton,

as though misfortune had befallen Hamilton, not himself.

Hamilton would have covered his surprise and his embarrassment with a blinding yet reassuring curtness interspersed with perfectly calibrated silences. Hamilton is ruthless and efficient. Hamilton is well connected and has a sinister charm. These, of course, are the minimum requirements for a cabinet minister. What made Hamilton a more potent force in this instance was his relative anonymity, his files, and the fact that in the end, he was accountable to no one.

My contention is that by this stage Hamilton would have made it known to our man that he had not confided in his superior, i.e. the head of MI5, or for that matter, in any of his colleagues. He would have betrayed himself as having exercised his considerable powers of discretion. He would have framed me as being safely in his pocket. Our man, of course, would have recognized that Hamilton was no political infant, that he was working towards a triumph of his own making. This was something he could readily appreciate. A new and vital partnership had been forged. There was a clear understanding that there was much work to be done if this partnership was to flourish. Now that Hamilton was sure that I had nothing to do with this new set of photographs the task to hand was to attend to the jealous boyfriend, Alex Simson. Blackmail was a fiendish crime. He would have to be discouraged from such a course. If, however, he just wanted Angela back, he would have to learn to be patient like the rest of us. He would have to wait patiently until she came back of her own accord.

An extraordinary meeting of the cabinet was called to discuss two urgent matters. The first, the renewed fighting in Bosnia. The second, the rapidly worsening economic crisis at home. House prices were continuing to fall. Inflation was low, but the national unemployment figure had reached above three and a quarter million and was climbing. A series of public sector pay strikes was imminent. The interest rate would have to rise yet again. There was plenty of work for our man and his colleagues if they wanted to stay in power.

The assembled press bombarded each minister with uncomfortable questions on the latter issue as each of them left Downing Street. Our man came forward for a brief television statement. He assured the public that the affairs of the nation were in safe hands. In these difficult times our goals had to be realistic. Our European partners were experiencing the same hardship.

'Thank you,' he said in conclusion, 'that is all I have to say. The Prime Minister will shortly be making a statement on these matters.'

As our man turned towards the waiting car Alex Simson pressed forward gently from among the crowd of correspondents and said in a low, confidential voice, 'What have you done with her?'

Questions were still being fired at the minister. Only he seemed to hear Simson's obscure question.

He lingered for just a brief moment, but it was long enough to commit the face to memory.

Judging by the way our man described it to Hamilton later, Simson was more patient than one could reasonably have expected under the circumstances.

I had an extraordinary meeting of my own, with Hamilton. We met in our motorway cafeteria.

'I have some bad news,' he told me, as though the misfortune was mine.

He gave me an edited account of his meeting with our minister. He passed me the information he had assembled on Alex Simson.

I was to take our man under my wing once again. I was to protect him. Hamilton would draw down extra funds for this job. 'Big fish — big expense account,' he joked mirthlessly.

I knew what he wanted right from the start. I knew what 'protection' meant. This wasn't to be a job guarding somebody's back. It wouldn't be enough to stand all night in the bushes or sit on a staircase with a pistol in my lap. This was a different kind of protection. Hamilton wanted me to recover incriminating evidence (i.e. the negatives and other prints that might exist, by whatever means). Then I was to kill Simson.

For a man who could so readily be deemed a threat, it was an enlightening meeting.

I had three options. I could say yes and do the job. I could say no and not do it. I could say yes and in doing so buy a little time to think. Working out the consequences of taking any one of these options was altogether more complicated.

I chose the third option. In the short term it was the safest for everybody concerned. I showed Hamilton the face I always showed him, but he must have caught the flicker of discomfort in my eyes that I could not suppress.

'You have doubts about this?' he asked with a cold underplayed incredulity.

'No,' I replied immediately.

'Don't you believe in the greater good?' he asked. He wasn't being facetious. This was a serious question, but in itself, it meant little. Everybody in the firm believed in the greater good. The question that mattered was, were you still part of that greater good?

'Yes,' I replied without hesitation, 'I believe in it.'

Hamilton gave me a vinegary look that suggested he was on this occasion prepared to indulge my brief moment of weakness, as reflected in my eyes, though he might dock fifty pounds from my fee.

He hadn't touched his tea. He had come straight from one of his committee meetings. He had had his tea there. Now, he was looking at his watch.

'Busy, eh?' I said. I looked out the window to the car park. It was ironic, I thought, I get to carry the body of a woman murdered by a cabinet minister with this man, but he would not so much as tell me where he gets his second-hand cars.

I was in a new and more dangerous game. I now realized that I was no longer an understrapper. I had ceased to be that the night we burnt Angela Richardson.

I went hunting Simson. I went to the offices of his newspaper. Mister Simson was out sick. I checked the local lunchtime haunts of journalists. I made discreet enquiries at the counters. Nobody had seen Alex today. I went to his flat in Finchley. He wasn't there. There was unopened post in the letter box. His shaving gear and toothbrush were missing. A chest of drawers seemed a little light. I looked for names, addresses and telephone numbers. He had taken his black book. There was nothing scribbled on scraps of paper, on the pad by the telephone, on the cover of the telephone directory. In the cistern I found a roll of negatives. Very good, Alex – what cabinet minister would put his hand in there? They were sealed in their container. The container was in a tightly knotted condom. A quick check confirmed the roll was part of what I was looking for.

I had a number for his parents. I rang them. The feeble voice of his father gave me a chill. I told him I was ringing from the news desk and that I needed to check some information with Alex but was having difficulty raising him. Could he help me?

The old man was surprised rather than suspicious. His surprise then gave way to embarrassment and frustration. Alex was letting down the family again, it seemed. Evidently, the father was less than impressed with his son's work.

He thought I might be ringing about Angela. Had I news of her? I could tell him in confidence, he assured me. I got the distinct impression that he felt his son was somehow to blame for her disappearance.

He had no idea where Alex might be. He was not expecting a call or a visit from his son but should the boy make contact he would pass on my message. There was a brief silence. Would it be enough to say that he was to ring the news desk immediately, the old man then enquired.

Yes, that would be the thing to do.

I drove to the West End, to see if I could get into the cutting rooms where Angela Richardson had been working. I assumed there would be somebody else doing her job now, somebody else cutting the same film, but perhaps I could find some clue as to where Alex Simson might be. I assumed the police would have held onto her address book and other personal effects besides, but I just might find a telephone number scribbled in chinagraph or a photograph of people or a place that might be identified. It was a long shot, but Angela Richardson was a missing person. Friends, colleagues and loved ones don't move the personal effects of a missing person. They leave everything as it is for a very long time. I needed something that had been overlooked, something that would point me in one direction.

I had to be careful. I didn't want anybody making a connection between me and Angela Richardson or Alex Simson. I didn't want anybody else committing my face to memory. I waited until I was sure the building was empty. I regretted buying a take-away. I regretted eating it. It put me in a bad mood. I started thinking that maybe Angela Richardson and Alex Simson had been in partnership, a pair, like Hamilton and me.

It was well after midnight when I made a move. The cutting rooms were at the top of the building. I had to climb a mountain of steep and narrow stairs that were covered in green linoleum and trimmed with metal grips. The rooms were a lot smaller and dingier than I had expected. The place smelt of stale tobacco smoke and sour milk. There were two Steenbeck editing machines, one in each of the adjoining rooms. There were strips of film hanging on pegboards from makeshift pegs. The pegs were opened-out paper clips that were fixed to the length of wood with drawing pins. The ribbons of film cascaded into bins lined with cotton. There were rolls of picture and sound on every available surface. Everything was marked and identified with chinagraph scribbles. I read what I could. I held up several strips of film at an angle to the beam of my pocket torch. In one I saw our man's head and shoulders. He was speaking to camera on the lawn in front of the House of Commons. I remembered a paler face with darker, more piercing eyes. All those little pictures of his head and shoulders looked the same as I followed him down into one of the bins where I lost him in the tangle.

I looked at other strips of film. Our man featured in many sequences. Backgrounds changed. In the foreground it was mostly talking heads. Our man seemed to have a lot to say for himself. The shots he did not appear in were shots of an impressive mansion, estate lands, masterworks of art.

HONOUR ALL MEN, that was the working title. It was scribbled on cans and on rolls of film and magnetic sound tape. Clearly, our man was the subject of this documentary. His work, his family history, his treasures.

So, this was how they had met? Our man had come up those stairs to this kip for a viewing of a rough assembly perhaps, or to test some piece of narration he had written to accompany the pictures or whatever the hell he might have to do. He had sat on that chair beside her. The producer and the director would have been too busy fawning over the minister to notice him looking at Angela.

I again recalled the look Angela Richardson had given me in that delicatessen. She would have caught our man looking at her instead of the screen. I was sure of it.

I stopped speculating. I suppressed my imagination. I tried to keep my mind clear. I resumed my search.

The police, as yet, had made nothing of the connection between our man and the missing Angela Richardson. Ironically, as I rummaged now,

I could find nothing that pointed to Angela's known relationship with Alex Simson.

Another missing person. I soon learned why Alex Simson had disappeared. Hamilton rang me to tell me that the old fool of a shopkeeper in Islington, having seen the crime programme on television, had decided that Simson had called into his shop on the fateful night and had bought the groceries listed on the receipt found in Angela Richardson's kitchen bin. He was, as he put it, 'almost certain' of this. Maybe Simson was in his shop that night to buy cigarettes or something. The police were sceptical, but it was enough to bring in Simson for more questioning. Hamilton was ordering me to do the job immediately, whatever the risk. The moment I set eyes on him I was to do the job. There was no time for elaborate arrangements.

Hamilton was worried. When Hamilton is worried things are meant to happen fast. He advises that crude methods are perfectly acceptable. All the while, he soothes with his cold charm.

I gave him my report. I told him I had Simson's roll of film.

'Why don't you take a trip down to Cornwall?' he suggested, 'he's sure to make contact with our friend. You can reel him in from there.'

It was the summer recess. Our man was spending a few days with his family in their house in the country.

'Cornwall's a nice place,' Hamilton advised, 'if you watch out for the holes.'

It was the logical thing to do. If Simson knew that the police were looking for him he would want to make contact with our minister again soon. He would want to conclude his game. He might telephone. He might visit. As yet, there was nothing to connect him with a cabinet minister who was spending a few days with his family on their country estate.

I could only guess as to what frame of mind Alex Simson was in. As I drove to Cornwall I tried to look at the mess from his point of view. How much of the picture did he have? What assumptions could he make? What was he prepared to do if, somehow, he had discovered the truth?

What was I prepared to do? I still had not decided. If I didn't do the job I would be a greater danger to Hamilton and his private plans, would I not? I would certainly be beyond the pale. I could see myself getting a visit from his chaps. There would be a different solution in the barrel of their syringe.

The sodden black paper sky seemed to peel off the dark landscape ever more quickly as I hurtled into the countryside. Sweat from my armpits made the handle of the Beretta damp and renewed some stains on the snug leather holster. I had had to get dressed up in a suit to see the minister. He was going to pass me off to his family and his minders as a parliamentary researcher. Hamilton had told me to bring a briefcase with a sheaf of paper in it.

The trousers of the suit now stuck to my thighs. My ugly mood had become a rage. If I was going to stick my neck out for anybody it would be on my terms. If the circumstances weren't right, if the risk was too great, I wouldn't do the job.

My foot got heavier on the accelerator. I cursed Hamilton. I cursed them all, everyone who had ever made me suffer for them.

I was stopped at the main gate to the estate by the local constabulary. I was expected and so was quickly on my way up the long drive. An early morning mist crawled out over the river bank, slithered across the meadow and wreathed the mansion in an ever-thickening band of opaque moist air.

I encountered just one minder. He watched me pull the car around on the gravel in front of the hall door. He was standing in the shadow of one of the gateposts of the courtyard. He had his hands casually dumped into the pockets of his waxed coat. Unlike myself, he had had his breakfast. He had just come on duty. He was relaxed, but alert. He automatically noted my car registration. He would be able to give an accurate description of me if it was ever needed. The others, too, would see me in due course. That couldn't be helped.

The minister greeted me as he would his star researcher. He introduced me to his wife and his three daughters. The eldest one was Angela Richardson's age.

I was offered breakfast. I declined. I lifted the

briefcase and said that I was anxious the minister saw the papers as soon as possible.

'Very well,' said the minister, with a hint of disappointment in his voice.

What a performance.

We went directly to his study. He closed the double doors behind him and stood waiting for me to turn. I didn't oblige. I walked to the window bay and struck a stiff pose, my gaze fixed on the meadow. The mist was already lifting.

'Has he made contact again?' I asked promptly over my shoulder.

'He rang. My wife took the call. I was out with my daughters. He left a message with her. He said he wanted to know where Angela was. I take it you haven't found him yet?'

'No.'

'What will you do?' He walked to his desk. The desk was the size of my car. He opened a box of cigars that cost as much as my car and offered me one. I was getting tired of people asking me how I was going to solve their problems. I picked out a cigar, rolled it between my thumb and forefinger, sniffed it, put it back in the box.

'I don't smoke,' I said.

'What will you do?' he repeated in the same measured tone. He was standing beside me now, looking out of the window, stretching the leather in his new shoes.

'Has he made a specific threat?' I asked.

'For God's sake man, what do you call the message he left with my wife?'

'An opening gambit,' I replied, taking my tone from his.

He scoffed.

'He sounds desperate enough for an answer to his question,' I admitted. 'He has approached you once in a crowd. I expect he'll want to confront you again. Alone, this time. He knows you're here. The police want to question him again. He won't wait long. Has he said what he wants?'

'I have just answered that.'

'You told me he hasn't made a specific threat. Has he said what he wants?'

'No. But if it's money, only a fool would pay.'

'In that event you have another solution in mind?'

'I don't think he wants money, at least not money alone . . .'

'We'll see.'

'What can he know?' For a brief moment I saw the minister wrestle with his fear. 'My wife,' he said, 'she didn't think anything of it. We get cranks. I don't know how the hell they get the number . . .'

There was a silence between us. He lit a cigar. He gazed out of the window at the meadow, puffing smoke. The mist outside had all but vanished. The cigar smoke gathered in the window bay.

'What sort is he?' he asked presently. He had regained lost ground. He was no longer gripped by fear. His political instinct and his intellectual powers were being brought to bear once again.

I finally turned and looked him squarely in the face. He liked that.

'He takes a good picture,' I said.

My curtness didn't bother him. He liked that, too.

'Look,' he said, 'is there anything you want me to do to facilitate your end of it?'

I was giving him the same blank look I gave Hamilton, but suddenly, I felt my mask slipping. 'I need some fresh air,' I said. I made my way to the door.

'I've been meaning to ask,' he said, calling after me, 'What did you do with her? I know it's none of my business, but I really do want to know.'

I had my hand resting on one of his fancy door handles. It was ribbed, like a grapefruit squeezer. When he asked about Angela Richardson's body I let the handle slip through my fingers. I straightened and turned. I narrowed my eyes without looking at him directly. He was grinning boyishly, as though I had asked him if he would lie to me. In spite of the grin his eyes were hard and aggressive, the way I remembered them. They wouldn't let go of me. He could read my thoughts. My mind flooded with the images he wanted me to share. He really wanted to know what Hamilton and I had done with Angela Richardson's body. He needed to know everything. He was a powerful man under threat. He was a politician.

I blotted out the images, but I could hear the rush of air in the furnace as it reached two hundred and ninety degrees. I could hear the mechanics of the grinder in motion.

'You're right,' I said, 'it's none of your business.'

He was not surprised by my rebuke.

'How is Brinsley?' he asked.

Brinsley? Who was Brinsley?

'Brinsley,' I said, 'Brinsley is fine.'

Of course – Brinsley had to be Hamilton's first name. I had not known the man's first name until now.

I hadn't forgiven Brinsley for organizing my chemical excursion to hell. What annoyed me most was his pretending that he now trusted me completely. He trusted me because, for the moment, he had no choice. Had I confronted him he would have set aside his mask long enough to burst with short-term commitment and that would have utterly sickened me. He must have known that I was aware of my precarious position and yet, we both continued to play the game.

'How many minders have you?' I asked abruptly.

'Three . . . in addition to the local bobbies, of course.'

'Three shifts?'

'Yes . . . you're not seriously suggesting that my life is in danger?' he asked, biting on his cigar. Seeing a cigar stuck in this famous face was disconcerting.

'I'm suggesting nothing,' I said and opened one of the double doors.

He reached into the top drawer of his desk and produced a hip flask. 'I need a walk myself,' he said.

I was looking at the family crest painted on an oak panel in the hallway when he caught up with me. The Latin inscription translated as TRUST IN GOD, HONOUR ALL MEN.

'Shall I show you around?' he asked.

'No thanks,' I said. 'I've seen enough.'

He started pointing out items anyway. We made two detours. In another window bay he showed me a chandelier in the shape of a galleon. In evening light, he explained, it appeared to be afloat on the river. It was a splendid house with a remarkable collection of fine art and furnishings. The minister revelled in his custodianship.

'They're making a film, you know,' he said.

'I know.'

'Bloody nuisance,' he declared.

The question about Angela Richardson's body hung over us. He brought it with him like a kite on a short string. Suddenly, he stopped in the doorway that led out into the courtyard. 'I say, you've forgotten your satchel. It would be better if you carried that with you.'

I had to carry the damn briefcase across the fields. It was a reminder that the minister had recovered fully from the shock of his own dirty work, that he had drawn a comprehensive map of his predicament. This map noted even the details of professional vanity to be observed.

He had put on wellington boots. No boots had

been offered to me. I was to make do with my city shoes. We trudged across the sodden meadow in silence. His two retriever dogs scouted ahead of us. Two minders kept pace with us, but at a considerable distance. He waited until we were a thousand yards or more out in the meadow before he spoke.

'That awful night . . . you said you understood . . .'

'Yes, that's what I said.'

'You can't have understood. Let me explain to you now what happened.'

'No, don't do that,' I said, but I *did* want him to explain. I wanted to hear him justify what he had done. As I said, he seemed to be able to read my thoughts for he proceeded to explain.

'I didn't mean to kill her. You must believe that. It was an accident. We had a dreadful row. She threatened me. She said she would go to my wife. Then she said she would go to the press. She was pregnant, you see . . .'

It was clear from the way he so carefully chose his words that I was supposed to fill in the emotional gaps.

'. . . None of this need have happened . . . none of it. In a fit of temper she raised a knife to me . . . I must have got it out of her hand . . .' His voice trailed off. He planted both boots firmly in the ground, his legs apart, as if there was a slight chance he might suddenly be swept off the planet. He took the hip flask from his pocket. He opened it and offered me some of its contents. I ignored his offer. I looked everywhere but directly into his eyes. I had seen what he had done. I had read Angela Richardson's face as she lay on the kitchen floor. I should have kept my mouth shut.

'Mister,' I said squinting into the light, 'you're a liar.'

He didn't know what I had seen. Hamilton certainly hadn't told him I had been taking photographs from a neighbour's roof. Our man, of course, was capable of keeping his mouth shut when it was needed. He had been called a liar before. He didn't fret. He was going to ask me again what we had done with Angela Richardson's body. I struck out on my own towards the river. I left him standing. His dogs came bounding back to him.

'Don't think I haven't suffered,' he shouted after me.

It had rained for much of my journey down from London. It poured again the following night. In the event, I *did* spend much of that night lurking in the bushes. I made a point of wearing the minister's raincoat and his wellington boots.

Alex Simson was a tenacious if predictable man, and circumstances dictated that if he was going to make another move he would have to do it soon. He would want a private audience with the minister, just as I had been granted. He would want to avoid the minders. If he was out there watching, if he was on the estate, he would have found the best vantage point. After all, he was a journalist handy with a camera.

The minders were sharp. I didn't want them getting him so I went out into the rain. I worked my way around the edge of the woods which marked the border of the front meadow on two sides. There was a rise one-quarter of a mile in front of the house. On my morning walk with the minister I had noted it as one of the key vantage points. From there a man with binoculars could comfortably keep watch on the front of the house, the entrance to the courtyard, the east side of the house and much of the driveway. Judging by his photographs, Simson was experienced at skulking in the night. The coppers patrolling the perimeter were unlikely to disturb him if he had successfully pentrated this deep into the estate. He would know to keep clear of the electronic surveillance in the immediate vicinity of the house and courtyard.

There was a strong wind blowing. The rain beat hard on the canopy of foliage. The air was cold and smelt sweet. As I advanced on the rise I sensed his presence up ahead of me. Would he hear through the downpour the drumming of droplets on the green waxed coat I wore?

You damn fool, Simson, I thought. I moved up towards the highest point on the rise so that I could come down on him from behind. I could not see far ahead of me. It must have taken me an hour or more to probe the margin of trees between the high ground and the meadow in front of the house. Then, I saw him. He was crouched like a pixie in rain gear at the foot of a tree.

In a short span of time I had witnessed a killing, I had assisted in the disposal of a murder victim. Now, I was to kill this man in cold blood. Wasn't this the job I had come to do? Wasn't this the way to get what I wanted, the way to get in out of the cold? Two shots fired at close range. He was a sitting duck. There was no risk. Nobody would hear two flat 'pocks' in this deluge, and so far from the house and from the gates.

I had the Beretta out and the safety catch off. I was close enough to do it, but I moved closer still. I had to be sure.

I don't like blackmailers. I don't like bad-tempered journalists who come pounding on the door when you're in the middle of dirty work. There wasn't anything I liked about Alex Simson.

I was as close as I wanted to get now and he still hadn't seen me. He was thinking too much about Angela or about himself. I had my feet planted firmly in the ground. I had a comfortable grip on the Beretta with my right hand. The heel of the pistol was resting snugly in my left. The job was as good as done.

How ordinary the act of murder seems to the killer, I was thinking as I stood there with the rain dripping off the end of my nose. How basic. Yes, that was what I had meant when I told the minister that I understood.

CHAPTER 7

DOING THE RIGHT THING

The critical moment had passed and I had not squeezed the trigger. I was standing on the edge of another black and bottomless hole, this time holding Alex Simson by the hand. The rain was washing the muddy lip from under our feet.

I gave a little flat whistle. He sprang up so fast that he ripped the back of his coat on the bark of the tree. I let him think I was part of the minister's bodyguard. I made him take me to his car. I insisted he take me via the route he had come.

It took us a hell of a long time to get to his car. He had sensibly parked it in a lane well clear of the estate.

'Where are you taking me? I've done nothing wrong. There's no need for a gun. Show me some identification. This is outrageous.'

I smacked his head. I pulled the drawstring out of his torn coat and I tied his hands behind his back while he spat all sorts of threats over his shoulder. He was frightened. Not as frightened as he should have been.

Then, he confessed to being a journalist. Didn't I

want to see his credentials? They were in his inside pocket. There'd be trouble over this, he promised.

I gave him another smack on the head. I really didn't like Alex Simson, but I had made my decision. Against all the odds, things were going to work out without my having to murder the bastard. That was the gambler in me speaking.

When we finally reached Simson's car I got him to open the boot. There wasn't much in it. A few car tools. A grip bag with a change of clothes. Some food. A manila envelope with a second set of the photographs Hamilton had shown me. I took the envelope and stuffed it into my coat.

This really scared him. He protested loudly. He tried to sound as outraged as he claimed to be.

'What size shoes do you wear?' I asked him.

'What do you mean, what size shoes do I wear?' he demanded. He was in a real panic.

I made a point of bending forwards, out of the light from the boot, to look at his feet. When he looked down at his feet I delivered a light glancing blow to his head with the heel of the pistol, and I bundled him into the boot. His shoes were a size smaller than mine, but mine were sitting in a corner of the saddle room of the minister's house. I wasn't going to drive all the way back to London in a pair of wellington boots. Wellington boots would be too clumsy for the pedals of a small saloon car. I squeezed into Simson's shoes. I didn't tie the laces.

The lane was so narrow I had to drive about half a mile to find a gateway in which to turn. I had to be careful turning. I couldn't afford to put a wheel into the ditch. Not with Simson unconscious in the boot.

It took me another half an hour to find the right road out of the area. For that half an hour I was lost in a network of narrow country lanes with high hedges and rough stone walls.

So. Here I was, doing the right thing. It didn't feel like the right thing. Once more I was driving through the night with that dry mouth I get when I sweat too much. Harry Fielding has scruples, a little voice was saying inside my head. That didn't feel right either. That was something that couldn't be kept secret. I would soon be the turkey in the boot and there wouldn't be a fool like me driving.

I hadn't driven far when Simson regained consciousness. I had stuffed his mouth and gagged him, but he could still make a noise through his nose. He began to batter the back seat panel with his bestockinged heels. He made quite a racket.

'Shut up, for Christ's sake,' I shouted over my shoulder, 'I'm doing you a favour,' but he kept on kicking. I had to pull in to the side of the road, open the boot and smack him hard on the head, the ungrateful bastard.

My life was going around in tight circles. Some people I had met were beginning to look like they were interchangeable. It was a disturbing observation. I began searching for ways to separate the experiences that were merging in my mind to suggest that I had let one event lead to another.

The sky was clear. It was raining somewhere else tonight. There was no moon. It had fallen out of the sky into one of Hamilton's black holes. Simson's car radio didn't work. There would be no chimes from Radio Moscow.

I needed to escape from the pernicious beat of my private and most urgent thoughts, but something poisonous Hamilton had let out of a box had got in behind my eyes and was burrowing through to the back of my head. It wasn't going to let me away with this. It was going to nest in the back of my head for a short time, then it was going to burst.

I wound down the window to let the wind beat on my face and roar in my ears. I began to whistle tunelessly through my teeth. I wanted a job where I could be happy making noise.

In spite of my whistling and the roar in my ears I could hear the insidious music of a motorway cafeteria. I could hear Hamilton lecturing me in a glum yet triumphant voice: 'Harry, old boy, we choose those who betray us.' I could hear him tap on the lid of his little box with a manicured fingernail.

It was a hell of a drive back to London. The engine overheated. I was forced to drive slower than I had intended. Simson regained consciousness and resumed his kicking. By the time we crossed Twickenham Bridge we had an escort of early morning commuters.

When eventually I pulled into the lane I had earlier decided upon, I was exhausted. The lane was deserted, just as I had expected, but the steady build of morning traffic was clearly audible from the streets beyond.

I opened the car boot. Simson, too, was exhausted. His head was spinning. He was completely disorientated. I cautioned him to be calm and to keep his mouth shut. I removed the gag and the mouth stuffing. I untied his hands. He sprang out of the boot like a salmon leaping straight into the jaws of a bear. I had to knock him back into the boot before he was properly on his feet.

'Who the hell *are* you?' he demanded in a whine. Then he threw up.

'Do you think I'm going to tell you after the beating I've given you?' I scoffed. 'I must have hit something soft.'

'By God, you'll pay for this,' he promised. Vindictive blackmailers make poor blackmailers, but that doesn't make them any less dangerous.

'I expect I will,' I said. I let him struggle out of the boot.

'I'll find you,' he threatened.

'No you won't,' I told him.

'I've seen you before,' he said, trying to fix me with a menacing stare.

'No you haven't,' I said.

'What happened?' he demanded. 'Why have you done this to me? What do you know?'

Now, I thought he was going to burst into tears.

'I know that the police who are looking for you will need shovels if you're not on a plane out of here today.'

This must have sounded somewhat melodramatic, but he knew I wasn't making a joke.

'Are you threatening me?' he asked hotly.

'Me? No. I'm protecting you.'

This must have sounded insincere, but it wasn't. He had a finger raised and was advancing unsteadily. I brushed his finger aside.

'Don't go back to your flat,' I advised. 'Borrow money from your friends if you must, and get out.'

'Who *are* you?' he demanded in a sudden rage. The finger was up again. I pushed it aside for a second time.

'I'm doing you a favour,' I said, kicking off his shoes. I went to get the wellington boots that were on the floor by the front passenger seat. Simson just stood in the lane in his stocking feet, holding his head in his hands. He was trying to make sense of what had befallen him.

'I could have left you with these,' I said, pulling on the rubber boots.

He must have caught a glimpse of the manila envelope stuffed in the inside pocket of my coat.

'You know something about those photographs?' he said in a deliberate and ominous voice. 'I want those photographs. Tell me what you know about the photographs.'

I straightened myself. 'Pal,' I said, 'you're a lousy journalist. Don't be the journalist with me.'

He persisted. He seemed to regain his physical strength and begin to think straight even as he spoke.

'You know something about Angela, don't you?'

he said. There was a dangerous mixture of pleading and anger in his voice now. 'What do you know? Tell me. Tell me,' he roared. He made a lunge at me. He let fly with his fists. He was, without doubt, an ungrateful bastard, and I told him so.

I had to smack him on the head again.

I put him in the back seat of his car. It wouldn't be long before he regained consciousness.

There was an Underground station not far away. I walked to the station in the minister's wellington boots. The boots forced me to move at what felt like an uncomfortable and unnatural pace. It was not a good start to my new life.

The red light on my answering machine was flashing. I let it flash. I decided that I was going to get rid of the answering machine. I wouldn't want such a thing wherever it was I was going.

I went into the kitchen. I stepped over the pair of wellington boots which stood to attention in front of the safe chair.

I was looking into my empty fridge when Missus Lamb knocked on the wall. I went to see her. She told me Maureen Talbot had called to my flat twice the previous night. The second time she called it was very late, Missus Lamb noted. I do believe she was sorry that I had missed this opportunity to avail myself of some comfort. She got me to move some of Lisa Talbot's belongings to what she claimed were more convenient places about her flat. That took half an hour or more. Then, I let her make tea.

'Here,' she said after she had swallowed her first mouthful, 'did you read in the paper – they think he's struck again – that serial killer. Nothing about it on the telly. Why do you think that is? Too many people killed in other places, is that it?'

The expression on my face must have suggested that I didn't care.

'It wasn't around here that he did it,' she added, 'but it might as well have been.'

I grunted. She got up with the teapot in her hand and went into her kitchen mumbling. 'I expect it will be on the news tomorrow when they know more about her . . .'

I didn't want to know about any more killings. 'They're hunting him, Missus Lamb,' I assured her belatedly, 'they'll find him.'

She re-emerged having added hot water to the pot. I had not yet taken a mouthful from my cup.

'I saved the paper,' she said. 'I'll get it for you now.'

I should have been working fast. I should have already implemented my escape plan. I should have been out of that whistling pile of bricks, but a strange calm had beset me. I didn't need a drink to steady my nerves. I didn't want a drink. I wanted to spend a week in the bath thinking about what I could do with the rest of my life.

I could see myself lying perfectly still in the tepid water, the Beretta with the safety catch released within reach. That was no way to spend a week.

I left Missus Lamb to drink her second cup of tea

alone. I went back to my flat. I rewound the tape and played my telephone messages. There were two. The first was from Maureen, ringing me the previous evening to say that she was calling at my flat to see me. The second was from my eleven-year-old niece. She wanted to remind me of her birthday. Then my brother, Peter, spoke in the officious voice he uses on the rare occasions that we speak. He wanted me to ring him. Our father was unwell.

I didn't return the call. Instead, I began to pack. I always keep a bag ready for a quick departure, but this time I wanted to take other things as well. I didn't know how long I would be away. While I packed I thought about my brother and his happy family. Happy against the odds, or, perhaps, in spite of them.

Peter had been another missing person. He had run away from our house in Leeds when he was seventeen and I was fifteen. He had gone out to the shops and had not come back. He had left a pathetic note. The police were not notified. It was a family matter. Our father said he would find him. When I came to London five years later my brother had made no contact with the family and our father had found no trace of him. I looked for Peter's face among the faces in the Underground and on the streets. I wanted to say to him that he should have been looking out for me, that he should have taken me with him. Then, one day, I saw him entering the Underground at Victoria. His face had changed, but I recognized him. I ran after him. I caught up with him on the station platform. I didn't get to discuss the bond that existed between us. There was other family business. Our mother was desperately ill. There on the platform I persuaded him to return to Leeds for a short time. He visited a week later. He acted as if he had just returned from the shops. He acted as if nothing had happened, as if there was no illness. I wanted to tell him that I understood why he acted in this way, but he left in the middle of the night. I could not bring myself to stay, either. Now, he was ringing me to tell me that our father was ill. Here was another of the ever-tightening circles that had been a part of a former existence.

The telephone rang. I lifted the receiver.

'Yes?'

It was Maureen.

'I hope you're ringing from Amsterdam,' I said.

She was still in London. She wanted to see me. She wanted to come over immediately.

'Why aren't you in Amsterdam?' I asked.

She would be going, she told me. She made some lame excuse that involved the man who was buying her sister's furniture.

'I don't want you over here,' I told her. 'Go to Amsterdam.'

She got in a taxi and came straight over. I had my bag in my hand when she rang the bell. I must have known she would come. I must have delayed my own departure by taking my time packing more than I needed, by standing vacantly with the bulging bag in my hand, for I experienced a strong sense of relief when I saw her standing on the other side of the door through the spy-hole. I felt my heart gladden at the sight of her face even before she turned from the bell panel to smile at the small glass eye.

The tabloid press still hadn't left her alone. They wanted photographs of her getting on with her life. Maybe even a shot of her visiting her husband's grave. Why had she not gone to Amsterdam?

I put down the bag. I quickly went to the boxroom to scan the streets. So far as I could tell she had not been followed. She rang the bell again. I opened the door to her. I embraced her. She said she wanted to stay the night. She looked at the bag in the middle of the floor.

'Were you coming over to see me?' she joked. I could see she was fretting. She was afraid I would leave her on her own. Why wouldn't she go to her friends in Amsterdam?

'I have to go away,' I said, 'I have some work to do.'

'You have to go now? Can't you go tomorrow morning?'

'If you've decided to stay in London why aren't you at work?' I asked.

'They've given me time off,' she said, 'to go to Amsterdam.'

I could tell by the way her face brightened she actually thought this would please me. The brightness remained but soon a curious playful nervousness was added. She let go of me. She scooped up the bag and carried it into the bedroom.

'Come on, Harry,' she said, 'we're safe in here.'

I think she meant safe from the press. I wasn't thinking about the press. We were anything but safe. I should have retrieved my bag and left her standing in the bedroom. I should have walked out into the street. I would have quickly found my bearings on the street had I had only the bag to hold, and not this woman's hand.

Long ago I had created a marshland around me and now, as I held Maureen Talbot's hand, I felt her sinking. There wasn't anything yet I liked about my new life.

We travelled by Underground. I took her to Jimmy Mo's pokey flat in Chinatown. It was hard to believe that Jimmy had such a thing as a spare room, but he did. It wasn't actually part of the family flat. It was a small room on the next landing. It was like my boxroom. In it he stored cartons of cigarettes for the vending machines he supplied and alcohol for the basement bar. He liked to call it his office, even though it had a bed in it, but no desk. For a month now he had been looking for another office, another place to store his goods. He and his wife, Pei-ti, were having another baby. Pei-ti wanted out of Chinatown. She wanted a house in the suburbs. He wanted to stay. He was prepared to turn his office into a proper bedroom.

His real name was Ta-so. His adopted name, his commercial name, was Jimmy, a name he very much liked. Barrett, my commercial name, was not something I could ditch. I carried it with me like a capsule of poison that I might need someday.

One of Jimmy Mo's legs is an inch shorter than the other. You wouldn't know it to look at him walk. Long ago he had learnt to walk on the ball of his foot. He had no need of a built-up heel. My eyes now fixed on the one unworn heel as he led us up the narrow staircase. Jimmy looked tired that night, and he looked older. That unworn heel seemed closer than ever to touching the ground. Jimmy doesn't complain, and he doesn't ask questions. That is why I have never really known what he makes of me, except that he counts me among his friends.

'You come down to eat,' he told me. 'Pei-ti is expecting you now.'

In the Underground train on the way here I had told Maureen that we would be safe from the press in my friend's flat. She didn't seem to care where we were going. Instead, she asked if I had again visited her sister in gaol. Though she tried not to show it, she was angry with me for having visited her sister without my asking her to accompany me.

'Are we just going to spend the night together?' she now asked.

'I thought that was what you wanted,' I said.

'Yes, well it is,' she snapped disconsolately.

People on the run and people hiding recognize each other for what they are and are apt to do foolish things to disguise the fact. I smelt the sweet musk of her body. I couldn't get close enough to her and still, she was sinking.

The light hadn't worked when Jimmy had thrown the switch. He had apologized and had gone to get another bulb.

'What a funny place to come to,' Maureen said to me. She pulled on the cord that was attached to the window blind. The blind went up like a sluice gate and light from a street lamp burst in. She turned to look at me as if it were her who had brought me here.

I didn't sleep well that night. Perhaps I should have spent the night gambling in the basement. Maureen slept soundly. She had enjoyed the family dinner. It had been an unexpected pleasure. It had been enough to make her feel safe for a short time. In the small hours I watched her sleep. Her face offered no clue as to her fears.

I got up at about 5.30 a.m. and went out for a long walk. I felt better once I was walking. I had already made up my mind that I would leave London by myself later that morning. I would stand over Maureen while she rang her friends in Amsterdam. Then, I would go to ground. I was buying a take-away coffee when I heard the seven o'clock radio news bulletin. Alex Simson had been found hanged in his police cell.

I had underestimated Simson's stubbornness in the face of danger, or I had smacked his head too hard. In any case, events were moving much faster than I had anticipated.

Part 3

DISTORTED

CHAPTER 8

HARRY ON THE RUN

The hinges of the main entrance door creaked louder than ever. The door now scraped the ground when it swung beyond fifty degrees. The place looked more run down, more dangerous. The window of the wooden telephone booth in the foyer had been broken. Vinnie had replaced the glass with a hideous amateur oil painting of a racehorse that happened to fit the frame exactly. It looked bizarre set in the door.

'Hello, Vinnie. How are you?'

Vinnie had his arm in a sling. While I frowned at that he looked at me with a little nodding motion of the head.

'The trouble with you English bastards is that the rest of us have to go through the whole song and dance again as if it's the first time we've met,' he said. 'What's wrong with you that yis can't pick up from where you left off? How am I?' he echoed in a mocking voice. 'How do I look? Do I look happy with this Jaysus arm which is broken in two places?' He didn't wait for me to ask what had happened. He carried on directly. 'Are the bookies after ya?'

I love Vinnie dearly. He is a good and loyal friend, though he would not admit it.

'I suppose you want a room?' he asked.

'Of course I want a room. Is there anybody new?'

'The same gang of gougers. Come on into the bar.'

'I don't want a drink.'

'What makes you think you're getting a drink? I'm getting a drink.' He was surprised by my not wanting a drink but, of course, he wouldn't show it.

'Fifty quid,' he announced as he led the way, 'that's as much as I can lend ya.'

'I'm alright for money,' I told him. He pretended not to hear.

'I've to see a man at six o'clock,' he said. 'There might be more after that.'

I was in Dublin. Nixer City, Vinnie called it. Everybody was doing a little job on the side, he had explained to me. Even the unemployed. 'Where do you want it?' was the question most commonly asked. In offering this information there was a sharpness in Vinnie's voice, but no bitterness. Bitterness, he had once told me, was a luxury he could ill afford.

I had taken the train from London in time to catch the night ferry to Ireland. I had made this journey many times before, when I owed money and could not pay. I had also gone there on some of the darkest of those shapeless days when I was afraid of being alone with the bottle. Vinnie's condemned hotel had been a safe place for me then. It would hide me again.

Vinnie ceased to take guests when much of the building was officially declared unsafe. Only the lounge bar was safe according to the City Engineer's Office. The lounge bar had been moved from the main body of the hotel into a new extension in 1958, the year after Vinnie had bought the place. Major structural repairs were needed now if it was to reopen as an hotel.

Vinnie had been a successful boxing promoter in England in the 1950s. He had bought the hotel with the money he had saved. It was a bad investment. It had provided an alternative way of life, but not a living. There was no money for repairs. By day it was a large, clumsy building thinly veiled by rusting Victorian ironmongery. It stood blind before the sea. The site was valuable. Property developers had repeatedly made offers. One of them would have it some day soon when Vinnie finally gave in. When that day came Vinnie would have no regrets. In the meantime, it was his private labyrinth which he shared with his small collection of misfits, none of whom he admitted were his friends. This was the one club to which I belonged.

The hotel had ceased to be an entity in itself. By night it bulged out of the side of the lighted flat-roofed lounge bar like some enormous abscess. I felt safe in this lump, switching lights on and off as I made my way on the sagging floors. The floors would have collapsed were they not tacked to lengths of hard-wearing carpet. I could lie on my bed or look out of my window or sit with the others. There was one upstairs room with a bay window that served as a living room. It contained much of what was left of the heavy mismatched furniture that Vinnie had bought. There was also a heater that ran on bottled gas. You became a member of the club by changing the gas cylinder.

I could sit in front of this gas heater or I could walk indoors or out. I could drink or I could sleep. I didn't want to drink. I longed to sleep. I had not slept well since I had come out of the nightmare Hamilton had arranged for me. My bones felt dry and brittle. My muscles ached. I needed to sleep. Sleep would clear my head of morbid thoughts. Even as I slept I would be moving forwards towards some kind of solution to my predicament, a solution that was of my making.

'Mind,' said Vinnie as we entered the lounge bar, 'she might be in here.' He did not say who, but, allowing for his familiarity, it could be none other than Teresa. Vinnie loved Teresa. I expect he never told her as much, not even when they slept in the same bed. She knew he loved her. Of that I was sure. There were times when his bluff manner drove her to distraction. She was fourteen years younger than him. She felt justified in her jealousy of what little attention he gave the chancers who took advantage of Vinnie's suppressed good nature. When he drove her to distraction she would tease and mock him. She would laugh at him in six languages then she would let fly with her temper. That accounted for the other nights, the nights they spent in separate beds.

Teresa wasn't in the lounge bar. The place was

deserted. It was more shabby than it had ever been. Vinnie went behind the bar and poured us both a large whiskey.

'Here,' he said handing me my glass, 'that'll make sure you sleep.'

I took the drink. I told him I didn't want to sleep just yet. I was trying to be polite.

'It's her birthday tomorrow,' he said. 'I'm going into the city to get her something. You can come with me.'

His tone suggested that this was a mild punishment to be inflicted on me for taking a drink under sufferance.

'Hurry up with that,' he then added, indicating the large measure in my glass. 'Remember, I've to see a man at six o'clock.'

As we walked along the sea front towards the train station Vinnie's empty jacket sleeve repeatedly slapped him on the back.

'I didn't remember her birthday last year,' he told me. 'I'll have to buy a new shirt now as well. She's been on at me to get a new shirt. I'm taking her out to dinner this time, you see . . .'

He was talking to himself as much as he was talking to me.

'So what happened to your arm?' I asked.

'Fell off the ladder,' he explained. 'Some bastard has opened a hole in the roof. They're trying to drive me out, Harry.'

He was telling me there was a conspiracy. He sounded like me griping with a few drinks in me.

'Anyway,' he said, 'I fell and broke the arm in two places. I told you that.'

We went to a city centre department store where he bought Teresa a thick, ugly necklace.

'She'll like this,' he assured me.

He then went to the men's department. At the shirt counter he found himself standing next to a man in his seventies. The man had a magnifying glass in his hand with which to read the size marked on the collar of a shirt. The sight of the old man raising the shirt collar to the glass made Vinnie uncomfortable. He leaned across, screwed up his eyes and hesitantly announced the size of the shirt. His assistance was not well received. The old man immediately put down the shirt, stuffed the magnifying glass in his pocket and moved away.

'I'm going blind myself,' Vinnie said to me, making light with his excuse.

Only then did I realize that he was deeply embarrassed by his broken arm. His accident on the ladder could be attributed to his failing eyesight. In spite of the glasses he wore on his battered nose, he could no longer do the running repairs on the hotel.

Vinnie was a big man. He had been a boxer in his youth, before becoming a promoter. He had never lost his heavy boxer's build. When he had chosen a shirt with an extra large collar he turned to look at the suit rack. There was nothing that would fit him properly off the peg. He wouldn't wear a suit that didn't fit right. There wasn't time now to get a new suit made. 'Any tailor will tell you that making suits for a boxer is a nightmare,' Vinnie had once told me.

The man Vinnie had to meet was to be found in a public house near the dog track. No money was forthcoming. We went to the dog track. Between us we lost everything we had with us except our train fare, Vinnie's new shirt, and the present for Teresa. We had walked some way from the track towards the station when Vinnie stopped. He was upset at having lost money on the dogs, but there was more to his black mood. As if he didn't get enough of it, Vinnie wanted a sea breeze on his face. He suggested we turn about and walk to the bay. It wasn't far. We could catch the train further up the line. The crimson lights in the halo on the statue of the Virgin Mary in Ringsend bus depot flickered on as we passed on our way. Vinnie took this as a bad omen.

We paused to look across the bay. There was still light. There was a Turkish moon in the sky. The green of the coastline was rich and dark. The bay was full of ink. The oil tanks in the docks looked like they were made of tar paper. Near where we stood a lamppost was humming madly. A group of corporation labourers dressed like pirates with pigtails and earrings were finally packing up for the day. For a moment, the prospect of danger seemed to me impossibly remote.

'Look at him,' said Vinnie indicating with his broken arm a man passing swiftly in front of us in a wheelchair, 'he doesn't need that.' There was no bitterness in his voice. It was as if he was secretly applauding the theft of a wheelchair.

Perhaps to Vinnie's eyes the bay beyond was just a blur. He was as blind as his hotel. I walked on towards the station. He stood still a moment longer, then he followed. The train carriage in which we returned seemed to be filled with interrelated families. Carbonated soft drinks were being fed to babies in bottles with teats. Everybody seemed happy.

We drank tea with Teresa in the kitchen. Then, we ate. Then, Vinnie went to help the lad he had serving locals from behind the bar. That night I didn't want to sit in the lounge bar or in the upstairs living room. I went straight to my bedroom. I slept fitfully. I didn't want a drink. My stomach was full. 'Damn this new existence.' I spoke these words into the dark. Panic had replaced the morbid thoughts in my head. I had looked at an English newspaper. I had read about Simson being found hanged in his police cell.

The following morning I woke in a sweat. I reached for my gun. Hamilton had been whispering in my ear in his soothing voice. He had been telling me not to worry, that he had made arrangements. He had already seen to it that I was officially listed as missing.

Foghorns were booming along the coast as if some great purge was about to begin. Vinnie was in the kitchen making breakfast. It was one of those days, he said, where we would all have to stoop to avoid brushing our heads on the grey porous ceiling that hung over the city. The statue of Our Lady of the Sea, set aloft on concrete pillars on the breakwater in the middle of the bay, had her head above the clouds.

It was unnaturally balmy. This was not the Dublin with which I was familiar. I ate breakfast with Vinnie. I gave him some money for my keep. I took the train into the city centre. I felt better walking in the crowded streets. When I was tired of walking I went to a pub by the docks. I sat in a corner facing the door. I forced myself to have a drink. I reviewed the events that had led me here.

I only remember having one drink. Half of that day went missing. I found myself sitting beside two old men in steel-capped boots. They were letting out a savage cackle of laughter, and I was laughing with them. The place was full of smoke. There were only a few old men in the bar. Others must have come and gone. When I stepped out onto the quay it was dark. The foghorns were groaning at half strength. It wasn't raining but the cobblestones were wet. The fog that had been choking the river mouth had crawled up the river and out onto the quays. The river was stagnant. I stood a while on the slippery rim. I could still hear Hamilton's voice in my ear. He was telling me I had nothing to fear. His chaps had done the job I had failed to do. Everything was again in order. He'd be docking another ten pounds, of course.

I heard heavy footfalls approach. I turned, and for the second time that day I reached for my gun. Out of the fog came a large man bearing a heavy sack on one shoulder. He was drunk. The sack was slipping.

I watched him as he threw himself against a wall to prevent the sack from falling. I watched him struggle to get his shoulder under it again. He advanced several paces further before the sack finally came off his shoulder and burst on the cobbles. Coal tumbled out, but did not roll far. I watched him circle the burst sack. I thought at first he was laughing. Then I saw that he was weeping. His task was now impossible. He abandoned the coal where it lay. He walked on with his hand over his mouth. His unsteady progress made me conscious of my own unsteady feet. I really didn't want another drink.

A short distance further along the quay a ten-year-old sprang out of a doorway and quickly fell in beside me, three of his strides to two of mine.

'Willya walk me to the bridge, Mister?' he said, 'I'm on me own.'

His hair was oiled. He was wearing a shell suit. His pockets were bulging with change.

'Is there somebody after you?' I asked.

'No. It's just in case somebody tries to kidnap me. You could hit him a dig.'

I asked him if he would hit somebody a dig if somebody attempted to kidnap me. He said that he would. I believed him. At the bridge he thanked me and, clutching the two lumps of change on his thighs, he crossed to the far side of the river and disappeared.

When I got back to Vinnie's place I telephoned Jimmy Mo in London. Had anyone been asking questions about me? I asked him. Had anybody come looking for me?

Nobody had, he told me, but the woman was still in his office. Maureen was insisting that I would be coming back for her. She had told Jimmy and his wife that she was afraid to return to her house. Jimmy was glad to hear from me.

Making contact was a foolish and a dangerous thing to do, but I was glad Maureen had not gone to Amsterdam. I rejoiced in her predicament. I despised myself for doing so, but I wasn't prepared to let her out of my grasp, not while I was afraid to be on my own without wanting a drink.

I told her I was in Dublin. That surprised her. I told her I wanted her to come to me instead of going to Amsterdam.

She said nothing about my leaving her cold in London. She said she would come directly. She cautioned me that I had better be where I said I would be. She didn't want to go to Dublin on any other account.

It was a foolish and dangerous thing she was doing, and I was glad.

At Dublin Airport there is a long glass-fronted corridor through which all passengers from London must pass. I was able to keep close watch from a similiar corridor of an adjoining wing with a long lens on my camera. I could see her make her way with a heavy piece of hand luggage. I trained the lens on each of her fellow passengers. So far as I could judge there were none of Hamilton's chaps following her.

I didn't meet her at the arrivals door. I had arranged

with her that we meet in a city centre hotel. She didn't bother with a taxi. She was a native. She knew to get the city bus that served the airport instead of the more expensive airport coach.

I had parked the hired car and was in position across from the hotel entrance when she arrived, struggling with her heavy bag. Nobody followed her into the building. Nobody waited outside but myself. I watched for some time before I went in after her. In spite of my caution, it was only when we embraced that I again felt that we both were in immediate danger. I got us out of that hotel foyer quickly. I drove us out of the city and along the lip of the bay to Vinnie's place.

'I didn't know you had a car,' Maureen said. 'I would have asked you to collect me at the airport.'

'I hired it just before I collected you,' I told her. 'That's what delayed me. I'm sorry.' I was trying desperately to sound like I was happy to see her, which was the truth.

'You're staying with friends here?' she asked.

'Yes. There's plenty of room. You don't mind?'

She didn't answer. She smiled instead. I didn't know what kind of a smile it was.

She gave the same smile when she saw Vinnie's hotel. 'This is a dump,' she said. She offered this observation as Vinnie himself might have done, in a matter-of-fact voice. 'Do we pay to stay here?'

'No – but I do give him something . . .' I said uneasily.

'I can get us a place to stay,' she said.

'Let's stay here tonight,' I said firmly.

We were still strangers.

Introductions were brief. Teresa was glad that I had somebody other than Vinnie with whom to spend my time. She warned Maureen that there would be no hot water for an hour or more. There are species of seasonal insects that can survive all year round in hotels. The constant heat from the extensive network of hot water pipes prolongs their lives. Such insects were not to be found in Vinnie's hotel. Vinnie's place was often colder inside than out. The plumbing was falling apart. There were damp patches that had started in the attic and had worked their way down into the foundations. No nixer quote was cheap enough for the repairs needed.

Vinnie welcomed Maureen in his usual gruff manner. He pretended that he had been expecting her, that she was overdue.

Then Maureen and I went upstairs. I entered the bedroom with military caution. She followed even more cautiously. Neither of us quite knew what we would do next. I cannot say that there was love between us. I can only say that in the passion we expended that night we cheated magnificently the forces that conspired against us. It was a strange kind of joy I experienced. Short-lived and without comfort.

I woke early, as I had done in our shared bed in Jimmy Mo's office. On this occasion, however, Maureen was already awake. She had been weeping.

'You don't want to be here?' I asked.

'I don't like this place,' she said.

'Do you really want to be with me?' What was I doing asking her a question such as this? Was I already looking to ditch her?

'I'm here with you now, aren't I?' she snapped.

The smell of the sea filled our room. I could hear the shouts of children playing on the sea front. Hamilton and his sordid private enterprise seemed a long way behind me. Perhaps that was why the sense of being in immediate danger had reasserted itself. I could not yet afford to think of myself as being safe.

'Can I ask you a question?' I said, '. . . about Frank.'

She shrugged. She was afraid to commit herself to answering.

'Why did you stick with him all that time when he treated you so badly?'

She looked hard at me.

'Why didn't *I* do it instead of Lisa, is that what you're asking me?'

'No.'

'I helped her, you know,' she said.

It was not difficult to see that she was lying to me.

'He did the same to her,' she said. 'What you don't know is that Lisa was having an affair with him. She did it because of what he had done to us both.'

Why was she lying to me about this?

The hot water promised the previous night had failed to materialize. I got out of bed now and went to the sink in the corner of the room and ran the hot tap.

'Did you sleep with Lisa?' she suddenly asked. 'Do you love her? She's not special, you know. What she did – what we both did – was wrong. Read the newspaper reports. You'll see . . .'

I didn't reply. I didn't know what to say to reassure her. I couldn't even tell her that she could have a bath. There was still no hot water.

She stiffened. Her spirit rallied. 'I don't like this place,' she repeated. 'We should both have gone to Amsterdam.' She was smiling at me again in her curious manner.

'Vinnie's brother has holiday cottages near Dingle,' I told her. 'They're right on the coast. There might be one vacant.' I had been there once. I had a clear picture of the place – the horizons, the approaches, the distance between points. I would only go where I had been before.

'Sounds like another spot I wouldn't like,' Maureen said vaguely.

'It's beautiful.'

'It'll piss rain.'

Vinnie had a blazing row with his brother, Matt, on the telephone. Vinnie always rowed with his brother. His brother wanted him to sell the hotel. It was an embarrassment to the family. Besides, Matt had a small stake in the property.

'He's building bungalows all over the shop,' complained Vinnie by way of introducing his absent brother to Maureen. 'He's destroying the country-side. It's blackguards like him that dig holes in roofs to let in the rain.'

In spite of the row, or, perhaps, because of it, Vinnie was able to arrange for us to have one of his brother's holiday cottages for five nights. Five nights was a long stretch into the future on my new calendar.

'Don't you want to call on your family in Dublin?' I asked Maureen as we drove speedily into the countryside.

'There's just my mother,' she said vaguely.

'Don't you want to see her?' It was safe to ask such questions now that we were free of the city.

'Lisa told you about our mother?' she asked. There was no vagueness in her voice now.

'She mentioned her.'

'A lot of old women here traipse to church every day. Not her. She's given up on religion. She stopped praying a long time ago.' The vagueness had returned, but in a different form. It was tinged with melan-choly. 'She goes to the criminal courts instead. She sits in the public gallery. She shouts. Sometimes, she weeps. She's obsessed with it. Her greatest scorn she reserves for those who plead guilty. I tried talking to her about our father. Did Lisa tell you about our father?'

'Yes, she did,' I said guardedly.

'Did she tell you how he beat our mother senseless and threatened her with a knife?'

'She told me he was violent,' I said.

'The old woman shouts and weeps for strangers in court,' she said with sudden bitterness, 'but she won't have a word said against our father.'

'He beat you and Lisa, too, didn't he?' I asked.

'Many times,' she replied.

'Perhaps your mother sits in court to atone.'

The sudden charge of bitterness in Maureen's voice was expelled as quickly as it had been embraced. The change had nothing to do with my last remark.

'Anyway, Harry,' she said suddenly smiling again, 'what do we care? What photographs have you to take? I want to know more about what you do . . .'

I gave her the same thin story I had given her sister. She wanted more than that. I said I would show her some of my work.

I thought about Lisa and Maureen's mother shouting and weeping in the public gallery of the central criminal court. I thought about Angela Richardson lying on her kitchen floor, and Alex Simson hanging in his police cell. I found myself glancing in the rear-view mirror as I pulled out of each bend in the road. Here I was again, driving out of a city into the night, sweating. I had put the gun in my bag for the night spent with Maureen in Jimmy Mo's. I had hidden it again when she had come to Vinnie's place. I didn't like keeping it in the bag. In a crisis it would take a long time to dig it out, to pull it free, to release the safety catch and fire. In a crisis it would be as useful to me as the steak knives at the bottom of the river.

The steering in this hired car was heavier than

I was used to. I take a long time to get used to a car. I thought about my own car which I had abandoned in front of the minister's house. The minister would have had Hamilton remove it. I didn't like to think of Hamilton getting my car. Hamilton had plenty of cars.

I thought about the minister's wellington boots standing to attention in my kitchen. Hamilton should have been given the boots instead of the car. The boots were better suited to his kind of dirty work.

I thought about Simson's photographs of his girl-friend, Angela, and the minister. If Simson had hidden a set of prints and they came to light, Hamilton would see to it that they were dismissed as fakes. I could see Hamilton producing manufactured photographs of Angela Richardson with each and every member of the cabinet to make his point. It was the negatives that mattered. Hamilton had Simson's negatives. I had given them to him in a former life. All Hamilton and his new pal, the minister, had to worry about was me.

'I'm cold,' Maureen said, 'could you wind up your window?'

I wound it up.

It was pitch dark by the time we reached Kerry. It was raining heavily. The narrow winding road heaved and plunged under the wheels. Some demon at the end of the earth had a firm grip on this ribbon of road and was making waves with a snap of its wrists. For a time, I was lost. I stopped the car. We could hear but not see the ocean. Both of us looked blankly at the map. We went on.

Eventually, we found the hamlet. I collected the keys from the local publican. The cottage was one of a group of modern cottages. Everything in it worked. There was a pint of milk in the fridge, tea bags in a glass jar, a large sliced pan on the sideboard. The place was still warm from the previous occupants, but there was a draught from under the front door. We lit a fire.

When I stood up from the grate I thought I caught sight of somebody standing momentarily at our window. I took my bag into the bathroom, dug out the Beretta and slid it up my sleeve. I went outside to investigate, but found no one. I peered beyond the small lighted areas into the darkness. The cold, fresh air filled my lungs and made me shiver. The rain pricked my face. I could hear the sound of the ocean and laughter coming from our neighbour's bedroom. I needed to relax. I went back inside.

Our fire was slow to catch. We were in bed before it had thrown out any heat. The smell of peat filled our nostrils as we wrapped ourselves in the bedclothes. Vinnie's brother may have been a cowboy builder and a philistine, but he furnished clean sheets.

This was the first night in what seemed like a very long time that I slept in a fully unconscious state.

143

Chapter 9

PROTECTING THE FAMILY

When I woke I was alone. There was a strong smell of her when I turned my face in the pillow. I looked for her shoes on the floor, but they were not there. I looked under the bed. There was a lot of dust, and no shoes. I got up and went to the kitchen. I called for her, but she was not in the cottage. I went outside. It was a bright, fresh morning. The sight of the mountains, the beach, the bay, knocked me back on my heels. The clatter of bottles being tipped into deep plastic crates drew my eyes to the pub at the bottom of the hill. I saw Maureen on the road in the distance. She was riding a bicycle. She was hunched over the handlebars in such a way as to suggest that the wheels were too close together. She was taking a run at the hill.

It was a man's bicycle. She had wanted to hire two, but there was just the one to be had. She had got it from the publican's wife. She didn't stop until she got to the top of the hill. Then, she walked it to the cottage. She insisted on parking it inside the front door.

I ate half the sliced pan for breakfast. Maureen was

content with two slices. I was sure she saw through my story. I was sure she saw my selfish motives in bringing her to this place, my shameless manipulation of her. And yet, I felt she trusted me. I didn't want to tell her anything more about myself.

'Lisa told me you were married,' she said. I couldn't recall telling Lisa that I had been married. In any case, the timing of Maureen's remark was uncanny.

'Yes,' I blurted out, 'I was married. I'm now divorced.'

She had been watching me chew every mouthful. She continued to study me carefully.

'Do you see her ever?' she asked candidly.

'No.'

'Is she with somebody else?'

'Yes.'

'Do you know him? I mean, did you know him before?'

'No, I didn't know him before.'

'What does she do?'

'She works in a laboratory.'

'What does he do?'

'He's a chef.'

'Are they married?'

'Yes.'

'You haven't had them over to dinner, then?'

'I told you, I don't see them. If they came to my flat he'd want to make the dinner. He'd use too many pots.'

'You don't mind me asking these questions, do you?'

'No,' I lied.

'You've not been over to their place, then?'

'The last time I was with my wife we had a row over a missing two-day-old take-away I had stored in the fridge.'

'I'm not surprised you don't like the chef,' she said after a brief moment of thought.

'I hate him,' I said. 'He's made a vegetable of her. He's boiled her soft.'

'They're right for each other. I can tell. Have more toast.'

She could see I was angry and that amused her. I swallowed the lump of bread that was in my mouth. I looked at her severely. That didn't bother her. She had more questions to ask, many of them more awkward than these.

'That bike,' I said with a cursory nod, 'you'll not get far on it.'

'It's a perfectly good bike,' she countered.

When we had finished breakfast we got on the perfectly good bike. Maureen reached between her legs and gathered the back hem of her skirt so that her bare legs were not resting on the cold metal of the back carrier. We got to the bottom of the hill where we had a puncture. The tyres were rotten. We laughed heartily, then marched the damn thing into the pub. Maureen got her money back. We then walked down to the beach. She held my arm tightly. She described how she had braved her husband's funeral. She was still desperately afraid that she was forever damned, that she would be hunted down and driven mad. We were better suited than my ex-wife and her chef.

The beach was virtually deserted. There was a solitary family in the distance. The father was dressed in his suit trousers and white shirt. A long tail of hair flapped at one side of his head. The mother was wrapped in a heavy black coat. The children were red and blue specks. A quarter of a mile beyond them there were two horse-riders and a dog. Maureen and I stripped to our underclothes and blundered into the water. She stood on a jellyfish, let out a shriek, but kept running.

'I can't swim,' she shouted excitedly.

We stood in the water up to our chests until our bodies were sufficiently numbed. She could tread water. We both trod water. She repeatedly sank up to her nose then came up spouting a mouthful of water. The way she stuck her chin in the air made me laugh. We rotated in the water. The bay was part of a larger inlet. We were surrounded by mountains. It was as if we had surfaced in a cold paradise. Maureen was needlessly concerned about our money and watches in our pile of clothes. She kept glancing in that direction.

'Look,' she said presently, 'there's somebody waving at us.'

With these words she had reached under my ribs and had squeezed my heart with a cold hand. I turned quickly in the water. I could see a man standing by our clothes. He had materialized in the time it had taken me to rotate three hundred and sixty degrees in the water. It didn't seem possible that a man could reach that spot from the cover of the marram grass in so short a time.

He waved listlessly at us. My heart pounded on the wall of my chest.

'Do you know him?' Maureen asked anxiously.

'Yes,' I said.

It was one of Hamilton's chaps. The big one, George. The one handy with a syringe. He was dressed in the same dark, hard-wearing suit he had been wearing when we last met.

'Who is he?'

I had inadvertently led the police to Lisa. Now, Maureen had inadvertently led this killer to me. It was my own fault.

'Somebody I used to work with,' I replied.

The Beretta was in the cottage. I was in the water. George could safely shoot us both and walk away. This was my only comfort as I rose in the water. Had his job been to kill me he would have already done so. I couldn't see George stopping short of completing his task, as I had done.

'I have to speak to this man alone,' I told Maureen.

'Who is he?' she persisted.

'Never mind who he is.'

'I promise I won't listen,' she said sharply. 'I'll stay here. I'll shout if I start to drown.'

'Get out of the water with me,' I told her. 'Don't go to the cottage. Go to the pub. I'll meet you there.'

'Wait just a minute . . .'

'Do it. Please, Maureen. I'll explain later.'

'We should have brought towels,' she complained bitterly as we waded out of the ocean.

'Barrett,' shouted George in greeting. 'What a coincidence.' He was grinning. He had his hand out for me to shake. 'Bloody cold, isn't it?'

I thought about catching him by his fat throat before I said a word to him, but Maureen made a point of being introduced before she went anywhere. She had given me a quizzical look when the name Barrett was used.

George shook Maureen's hand weakly. 'Very pleased to meet you, Miss,' he said. 'I've heard so much about you. Bloody cold in that water, I'll bet.'

Maureen gathered her clothes and left abruptly. George continued to grin at me. She's a nice colleen,' he said.

'Where's your friend, the short bastard?' I asked. 'Watching from the long grass, is he?'

'Who, George?'

'Oh, he's called George, too?'

'Yes, he is.' The grin broadened. 'George is on another little job.'

'And what's your job today?'

'You're shaking, Harry . . .'

'Haven't you noticed? It's bloody cold.'

'Mister Hamilton wants a word.'

'Does he?'

'He said you were on holidays, but he needs to speak to you. He has some news for you. He asked me if I would contact you. I said, "Well, Mister Hamilton, that's a coincidence, I'm about to take my annual leave," and he said, "George, all you have to do is get Harry to give me a ring." So, here I am. On holidays. Give Mister Hamilton a ring, Harry. If you find that he's away on holidays, ring your brother.'

He turned his back on me and walked towards the dunes. His slow, deliberate gait mocked my stupidity and my blindness.

I picked up my clothes. I began to run. I caught up with Maureen on the road.

'I have to leave, right now,' I told her.

'Who the hell was he?' she demanded. 'What does he know about me? You've been lying to me – Mister Barrett.'

'Listen to me . . .' I took her by the arm. She pulled away violently.

'I want you to leave. I want you to go to Amsterdam immediately.'

'I don't take orders – certainly not from a stranger.'

I took hold of her arm again. Again, she wrenched herself free.

'You don't understand . . .' I protested.

'Lisa told me to keep away from you. She said you were a liar. She said you were dangerous . . .'

She wouldn't stand still. She tried to get past me. I got a tight grip on both her wrists. I put my face in front of hers.

'I'm in trouble. Deep trouble. Can you understand that?' I was speaking with my stomach muscles. I was speaking through clenched teeth. My rage frightened her, but she did not flinch. She looked straight into my eyes.

'I understand,' she said.

How could she have understood?

'I must go back to London now. Give me a number where I can contact you. I'll ring when this is over.'

'What have you done?' she asked in a small voice.

'Nothing,' I said, 'I've done nothing . . .'

I realized how hard I was squeezing her wrists. I must have been hurting her, though she made no protest. I released her.

'You'll tell me all about it later?' she asked in the same small voice. 'You'll show me pictures?'

'Yes,' I said, 'I will. Give me the number.'

She slapped my face. I turned my back on her and began to climb the hill.

'I can help you,' she called after me in an urgent voice.

She had looked deep into my eyes. She had seen the violence in me. I was forced to admit to myself that this was what had drawn her to me. She would help me because this was something she believed she did understand.

I was filled with rage and self-loathing. There was no such thing as a new life.

I hadn't touched the bottle of whiskey I had brought for my brother, Peter, and his wife, Sarah. I had brought the match of the grubby shoe from under my wardrobe. They did have a dog. A vicious beast.

'Here,' I said the moment Peter opened the door to me, 'that's for you. This is for the animal.'

'You're drunk,' he said knocking the bottle aside.

We were both in a state of anguish. I was having to pretend that I didn't know what had happened, that this was a casual visit. I had to look into my brother's pained eyes and raise my eyebrows in surprise. It was a sorry test of my sanity.

'Where the hell have you been?' he growled. 'I've been trying to contact you. I've had the police to your flat looking for you. Rachel is missing.'

I had listened to all my brother's distressing messages on my answering machine. I had tried to contact Hamilton but access to him had been denied me. He wanted me to sweat. He wanted my worst fears to prey on me.

There was a plain-clothes copper in the living room. Peter pushed me into the kitchen.

'Where's Sarah?' I asked.

'She's out with the police looking. We're taking it in turns. One of us has to stay by the phone. Oh, Christ, Harry . . .'

'Peter, she's probably taken off by herself. We'll find her . . .'

'You can help,' he said clutching my arm. 'You can help us.'

My brother knew that I worked for the security services. He did not know on what basis. He saw me as some kind of Whitehall rat with a plumber's tool kit. I spied on terrorists. I protected powerful people. I was a James Bond.

'She's been kidnapped . . . I know it . . .'

'How long has she been missing?'

'Eighteen hours, now. She didn't come home from school. Christ,' he bellowed, 'the school is only up the street . . .'

The copper came to the kitchen door. I signalled that he need not offer assistance. The doorbell rang. A woman's voice could be heard through the door.

'Those bloody neighbours,' Peter said turning angrily on his heels.

'I'll see to it,' said the copper.

'Oh, God,' said Peter turning the same anger on me, 'somebody has taken Rachel. Do something, Harry.'

I was having to put on an act. The drink wasn't part of it. It wasn't difficult to measure my brother's distress. He was swinging his head to and fro. I couldn't bear to watch him do this. I caught his face between my hands. I swore to him that I would get Rachel back.

'You can get money if we need it, Harry, can't you?' he said in a desperate, conspiratorial whisper.

'We'll find her, Pete,' I told him. 'We'll get her back whatever it takes.'

'Christ,' he wailed, 'you're drunk.'

'I'm not drunk,' I insisted. I still had the damn shoe. It was under my arm. The dog was out roaming the streets. Peter laughed hideously now that he saw the shoe.

The copper kept the neighbours out. He partially opened the hall door.

I rang Hamilton's number repeatedly.

'Sorry, Mister Barrett,' came the repeated reply, 'Mister Hamilton is still unavailable. I *have* told him your call is urgent. He *has* said that he will return your call as soon as possible.'

I thought about going to look for him, but knew that such a move would achieve nothing. I would not get to him. He wanted me to sweat. There was nothing practical that I could do. I would have to go back to my flat and wait.

Missus Lamb came out of her flat when she saw me enter the building.

'They've caught him,' she announced triumphantly.

'Who have they caught, Missus Lamb?' I asked. I didn't want to talk to her. I wanted to squat in a dark corner and plead with the telephone to ring.

'Don't you ever read the newspapers? It's been on the radio, too . . . the killer, they've arrested him.'

'They're sure it's him?' I asked wearily.

'There's been no name released, no picture of him yet, but it's him alright.'

'I'm glad you're sure,' I said. I asked her if anybody had called at my door in my absence. She told me that the landlord was creating a fuss over Lisa Talbot's furniture. Nobody had come to collect it. He was threatening to dump it in the street. Missus Lamb wanted me to come into her flat to rearrange the stored goods once again. I told her that I had urgent calls to make. I would move whatever she wanted another day.

'Oh here,' she said, remembering, 'there was one caller. He left something sticking out of your box. I took it in.'

She insisted that I come into her flat and sit down. She made a little ceremony of handing over the small parcel. She then went into the kitchen to make tea. I got up and left. Before I closed her door behind me I shouted to her. I told her I had to make my telephone calls. When I had closed my own door I ripped open the parcel. It contained a dog's collar, nothing else. The disc on the collar bore the name of my brother's animal together with my brother's telephone number.

I rapped on Missus Lamb's door.

'The person who delivered this – what time did they call?'

'Middle of the afternoon . . .'

'A man?'

'Yes.'

'What did he look like?'

'Well,' she said, struggling to summon an image, '. . . he was polite . . .'

'Was he small? Bald? Dressed in a suit?'

'He was small, but he was wearing a hat. It's bloody cold, in case you haven't noticed . . .'

I must have given her a strange look.

'He *was* wearing a suit . . .' she quickly added.

She didn't want to disappoint me. 'He polishes his shoes . . .'

The kettle began to whistle in her kitchen.

'It's almost six o'clock,' she said, 'we can watch the news. We can see about this killer . . .'

'I must make my calls,' I told her, cutting her short.

For a long time I sat on a hard chair in the boxroom with my head clasped in my hands. My eyes repeatedly rolled in my head to fix on the wellington boots in the kitchen. The dog's collar lay on the table above. The dog was dead. My niece was in a safe house, drugged. Little George was stroking her hair. He, too, was waiting for a telephone call from Hamilton. That which had poisoned my life I had let loose on my family.

I tried to breathe evenly. I kept both my feet planted firmly on the floor. The pressure I brought to bear on my skull made me see stars the size of my hands spin before my eyes. Hamilton whispered in my ear that he would put everything right. He would protect the innocent with the same diligence he employed in protecting the guilty. I was afraid that I was going mad.

Hamilton rang at 11.00 p.m. He claimed he was returning the last of my many calls. He pretended that he was nothing more than irritated with me. He was short, as if he had his kippers on the grill.

'Whatever you want me to do, I'll do,' I told him.

'I've assumed that from the outset, Harry,' he said, 'and I've been disappointed.'

'For God's sake, send her back.'

'I've heard about your niece. I had to send George to find you. I want to help. I can meet you—'

The whispering in my ear was becoming a reality. I interrupted him.

'Please . . . you know where you can find me . . .'

'Whatever the firm can do . . .'

'Send her home, Hamilton.'

'I've had a word with the detective in charge of the investigation . . .'

'Please . . .'

What did he want of me? He didn't want rid of me. He wanted to break me. He wanted me to submit absolutely to his will. Ours was truly another of his special partnerships. At that moment there was nothing that I would not have done for him. He wanted that to be a permanent arrangement. I could undertake tasks he could not give to his two Georges. I need be accountable only to him. In time, I would come to respect him, whatever was required of me. In this instance, I was required to play his cruel game.

Rachel was brought home by detectives early the following morning. She was completely disorientated. What little she could remember of her abduction and her incarceration was a jumble. The drug she had been given made her sick now that she was coming out of the stupor. She had been let out of a van on Savile Row and told to go into the police station and ask for her dad.

My brother rang with the good news. He thanked me. I told him that I had done nothing to deserve his thanks. He refused to believe me.

There was no answer when I rang the Amsterdam number. I rang Vinnie's number in Dublin. I wanted him to see if Maureen was still in the cottage. A detective answered the telephone. He spoke in a slow, cautious voice. He would not give me details. He would only say that there had been a fire in the hotel, that Vinnie and his wife were recovering in hospital. He gave me a telephone number for the hospital. I could see this detective standing incongruously in the kiosk in the blackened foyer, the painting of the racehorse punched out of the window frame.

Teresa had been badly burnt. Vinnie had gone back into the blazing building to get her out. He blamed himself for her burns. He blamed each and all of the property developers who had approached him for the fire.

I knew better. This was part of my punishment. Big George had completed another of his tasks. Hamilton had set fire to somebody else. It was I who was to blame for Teresa's burns as surely as I was responsible for the anguish my brother and his family had suffered.

CHAPTER 10

CHINATOWN BEAT

I met Hamilton in a motorway cafeteria. He was late. That aside, everything was meant to be as it had been when I was his understrapper. 'Harry,' he seemed to be saying to me, 'we have succeeded in our sacred mission to protect the minister.'

When he sat down opposite me and declared that everything was in order my heart dropped like a rock descending a chimney. I looked at the bowl of porridge he had brought on a tray. He studied my expression.

'You don't like porridge?' he asked. 'There can't be many who don't like porridge.'

I raised my eyes slowly. I let him read my mind.

'Look, Harry,' he said in a perfectly reasonable tone, 'I need a man like you. I need somebody on the outside, as it were.'

'To do your dirty work?'

'Precisely.'

His candidness was shocking in spite of my knowledge of the man.

'You make me sick,' I told him.

'Indeed,' he replied mildly. For a moment he

turned his full attention to his porridge. He poked at it, then he ate a spoonful. He unfolded the newspaper he had brought and spread it on the table. He moved my empty cup and saucer to make room. 'I see they've arrested somebody for those killings . . .' he said.

'One of your chaps?'

Now it was his turn to raise his eyes, but he thought better of it. He continued to scan the newsprint. 'I'll not be asking you to kill anybody,' he said. 'I know how you feel about killing . . .'

'Do you?'

'There's no point in my looking for a combination of skills not to be found in one person,' he said, narrowing his eyes mockingly.

He ate more porridge. He spoke again presently.

'I've called you here early today, Harry, to tell you that I recognize your loyalty and your scruples. You will, of course, recognize the same in me. I will not see a good man go down if I can help it. I see the same quality in you. Now,' he said in a slightly deeper voice, 'I have a job for you . . .'

The job was to photograph some damn judge who liked the company of homeless boys. Hamilton promised there would be more money in future. He gave me bunk about this one being a delicate operation. In fact, it was a job for someone from the firm. Somebody just out of the nursery. He could have given it to Winston. Winston could have done the job with a Box Brownie.

My car was sitting outside in the car park. Hamilton

had driven it to this place himself. He had one of his chaps follow him in his Rover.

'You *can* start it, I take it?' he enquired. 'You don't need my key?'

Hamilton could rely on me. I did the job. My humiliation was complete.

I returned to Dublin briefly to visit Vinnie and Teresa. Teresa was still in hospital. Vinnie's brother had put him up. Vinnie's cronies from the hotel had scattered without trace. He asked me if I thought it might have been the gas fire that had started the blaze after all. I said that I was sure it was the case.

His brother would not row with him. He couldn't sit still. We walked the pavements of the unfamiliar suburb where his brother lived. Somehow, Vinnie had managed to stay on his feet.

'The necklace is gone,' he told me. 'the suit and all . . .'

'Never mind, Vinnie,' I said.

'Don't be asking me for money now, do you hear?'

'I won't,' I assured him.

'You're a good friend, Harry,' he said.

'When can we see Teresa?' I asked.

'We'll go in in an hour,' he said. The time was fixed in his mind.

'Shall we go back to the house first?'

'She won't let me bring her anything.' He hadn't heard my question. 'Isn't that strange? She says there's plenty there already.'

Plenty of what? He didn't say.

'Let's go back to the house. We can call a taxi.'

'They tell me she'll be alright in the end, Harry,' he went on. 'Can I believe them?'

'Yes,' I said, 'you can.'

We turned about face.

'I think it was the gas fire after all . . .' he said.

The shapeless days that followed were like nothing that had gone before. I confined myself to my flat. I lived on biscuits and tea. I hammered on the wall with the billiard-ball each morning. I needlessly cleaned the Beretta each night. I looked to gather strength in the darkness and the silence.

I climbed out of the hole that I occupied to attend my niece's birthday party. It was a special day. A day on which we could give thanks for her deliverance.

My brother and his wife wouldn't let her out of their sight for a moment. Rachel had recovered well from her ordeal. She had forgotten as only a child can. I watched her press her head into the soft belly of her grandfather's clean white shirt. The old man was ill, but he would not have missed this day. He stroked her hair. She had her arms around his middle, trying in vain to get her hands to meet. I remembered my appeasing this man who had beaten us. He had also forgotten, but in a different way to the child. I looked to my brother. Had he, too, forgotten? If he had, there would be nothing to forgive.

I was forced to admit that I could scarcely remember much of my unhappy childhood. I knew that I would speak to the old man now without reproach.

I knew that I could conceal my bitterness with ease. I knew that I could deceive him utterly. I could make him think that I was seeking his approval.

I was more uncomfortable with my niece than with the old man. I wanted nothing to do with the pains of growing up. I could offer her no guidance, no real protection. I could only take solace in the happiness evident in my brother's family. That was something I could celebrate with an embrace such as the old man now gave Rachel.

I thought I might drive past my flat. I thought I might go to the worst dive I could think of. Then, I thought maybe I should eat instead of drink. Maybe I should eat first and then drink. I pulled into the adjacent street and parked. I got out and walked around the corner. I looked in the window of my local cafeteria. I saw Missus Lamb. She was seated near the front. Her face lit up when she saw me. She beckoned me.

I had a cup of tea with her. I watched her eat a plate of chips. She was anxious to relate to me a newspaper report of a solitary bag-snatcher who was operating in the city. This villain lay in wait at traffic lights. He would select a lone woman driver and knock on her window. When the window was partially opened he would release a live rat into the car. The woman would evacuate the car and he would snatch her bag from the front seat or the floor.

I agreed that this was too much for one person to have to suffer so that another might benefit by a few pounds. That made Missus Lamb feel better. She was afraid that such an attack would no longer evoke a sense of outrage.

She told me that some dealer had finally collected the heavy furniture from Lisa Talbot's flat. It had been repossessed. When Missus Lamb had finished her chips she confided that she had visited Lisa in gaol. She asked if I would care to come with her on her next visit.

I got back into my car and I drove to Chinatown. I had decided that I wasn't hungry. I went to Jimmy's den where I had a couple of stiff drinks. Jimmy was nervous about something. He wouldn't stay any length of time to talk. I started feeling sorry for myself. There were others for whom I should have felt sorry but I had been trying to forget about them.

I had another stiff drink, then I joined the game in the back room. I lost a pocketful of money, then I won back the same amount. That didn't seem right. Somehow, I had been cheated.

I was tired. I had had too much to drink. I didn't feel lucky. I was sure the coppers would have pulled me in had I attempted to drive home. I didn't want to go back to my flat. I wanted more drink. I told Jimmy that I wanted to sleep in his office. He didn't like the idea. He got very anxious. He told me I could sleep on the couch in his living room.

When Jimmy had finally locked up we walked the short distance to his flat. As we approached the entrance to the building he looked up at his windows. The light was on in his office.

On this occasion he didn't offer me anything to eat or drink. Nor did he sit and smoke a cigarette and talk with me about his business and his family. Instead, he got me a pillow and a duvet and left the living room with a formal 'good night'.

I lay on his couch, but I couldn't sleep. The drink had me thinking the place would burn down if I closed my eyes. I listened to the noises from the street and the building's plumbing works. I heard Jimmy row with his wife in strained whispers. It must have been about five o'clock in the morning, when all else was quiet, that I heard a car pull up in the street below. A short time later I heard a disturbance upstairs. I swung my legs off the couch. I got up and I went out onto the landing. I was sure the noise was coming from Jimmy's office. I quickly and quietly descended the staircase until I turned into the flight of stairs that led to the street. There, I stopped and crouched. I could see that the door to the street was open. I could see the tail end of a car, the exhaust pipe pumping out fumes. My suspicion was confirmed – some kind of a raid was in progress.

I climbed the stairs. When I turned onto the landing where Jimmy's office was located I heard the unmistakable sound of flesh being beaten and the muted nasal cries of a gagged victim. I carefully pushed open the door. I saw this one man strike the woman he had partially bound. She was kicking out with her feet. Her hands were tied behind her back. A wide strip of sticking plaster had been slapped across her mouth. I recognized the woman instantly. She was my tall friend from the restaurant. Her attacker was trying to get her out of the room, down to that waiting car. When I came through the doorway he was hitting her with his fists. Something burst inside my head and made me cry out. I let him turn towards me and straighten before I fired. I shot him twice. I shot him squarely in the chest. Two holes close together, like a pair of eyes. I heard the car down in the street pull away on screeching tyres.

I had finally got to protect somebody.

I looked at my friend. She had stopped squealing through her nostrils. She was crouching in a corner. Her eyes were wide with terror. They were fixed on me. Even when her attacker kicked involuntarily on the floor in front of her, her eyes remained fixed on me.

The gunshots must have woken everybody in the house. Jimmy came upstairs with a wooden club in his hands. He was first on the scene. He got me out of the building into a laneway without my being seen. Jimmy had been hiding the woman from her family in London and from her attacker. Her attacker was her first husband, to whom she was still married. She wasn't Chinese, as I had thought. She was Vietnamese. She had married this man in Hong Kong and she had fled from him. Being her deserted first husband didn't seem to me to be an adequate excuse to beat and kidnap her. Shooting him was just a little more than he deserved. I could live with that.

I had shot him twice. I had killed the man. I had to ditch the gun immediately. I wiped it clean of fingerprints. I dropped it into one of three tall restaurant bins. Had I not been drinking I still would have shot him. Had I not been drinking I might have made good my escape. As it was, I got no further than the mouth of the lane. It was my misfortune that there were coppers in the area when they got the report of a shooting over their radio. I virtually ran into them. It was the same two plain-clothes coppers who had come for Lisa in the restaurant. Chinatown was their beat. I can't think why I thought I might get past them.

I could hear police horns in the distance, or was it the sound of an ambulance? I looked back down that lane as the handcuffs were snapped on my wrists. I don't know what I expected to see. Perhaps I was hoping that I would see Jimmy lead my tall friend away from the mess.

I kept my mouth shut. They kept asking about a gun. A space had opened up in my head. A non-conductant space. Perhaps that explains why I heard none of their other questions.

They made no reference to Lisa Talbot's husband and my trip to the woods beyond Beaconsfield. They were saving that until later. They were concentrating on this Chinatown slaying. They were sure I had had an accomplice. A driver who had panicked when they saw the unmarked police car. They were not prepared to accept that this was a simple matter.

What was I to tell them? Was I to tell them that I had a sacred mission to protect the innocent?

No doubt they had found the Beretta. They knew that I had killed the Chinaman. They wanted a confession. I expect they were asking about my relationship to the dead man's wife.

When they saw that they were going to get nothing out of me they organized an identity parade. There were ten others and a sergeant in the room when I entered with my court-appointed solicitor and two detectives. These ten had been instructed to have no communication with me. Their names, addresses and their ages had been taken, together with a note as to their dress. The sergeant writing the details had ensured that they all had their jackets off and their sleeves rolled down in keeping with the way I was presenting myself. I was entitled to make reasonable objection to any person appearing in the line-up on the grounds that they bore no resemblance to me. I scanned the faces. Many seemed too young, too fresh. None of them looked like me. I was formally asked if I wished to lodge an objection.

'Let's get on with it,' I said.

They let me arrange the order of the parade. I put myself between two coppers. Most men in the room were in awe of me. The tension made me behave like a criminal.

'Hands behind your backs,' I ordered.

Those who had not already adopted this posture now clasped their hands behind their backs.

My tall friend was behind the two-way mirror. It

had to have been her. I was sure nobody else had witnessed the shooting. With the evidence already accumulated they weren't about to have a parade for somebody who had merely seen me leave the building. What did my tall friend make of this stranger who had shot and killed her violent husband?

I knew that at this moment I should have felt something – fear, shame, remorse – but I felt nothing. Instead, I marvelled at my life. My tall friend must have been terrified and confused. Not confused enough, however, to prevent her from making a positive identification.

They hadn't made up their minds on the motive. They had only begun to dig. A charge of murder would be the safest in the meantime.

The fear came soon enough. Being banged up in a police cell got me thinking straight again. As straight as the crooked path on which I travelled would allow. Hamilton was cautious and he was thorough. He liked to use tried and tested methods. He knew that I would be tempted to tell my tall tale to get myself out from under this murder charge. I thought about Simson. Simson with his tongue sticking out and his eyes bulging. Simson with a blue face.

It was 4.00 a.m. when I heard the footfalls in the corridor. I got off the bed. I stood with my back to the wall facing the steel door. This cornered rat was going to spring. Harry boy was going to tear apart the biggest one to come through that door. Harry was going to shout for help. Harry was going to scream blue murder.

There were two of them and a police sergeant. The presence of the sergeant was reassuring. Nothing would happen while he was with us. Some arrangement would have been made if anything was to happen in the cell. I hadn't seen these two before. They were ordinary chaps. Fresh-faced, well-heeled, public school types. Getting up at 3.00 a.m. was no bother to this pair. It was good for the character.

One had a speck of shaving cream on an ear lobe. The other didn't need to shave.

'Look here, Harry,' said the one with the shaving cream, 'you've to come with us.'

Clearly, the sergeant had been instructed to ensure that ours was a speedy departure from the station, but he wanted another close look at me. He managed to walk me to the waiting car in spite of my close escort.

'Where are we going?' I asked the driver as we sped away up the wet street. He was another fresh-faced twerp.

There was, of course, no answer. He managed to look in the rear-view mirror for traffic without making eye contact with me. I sat wedged between my two new pals. I smelt of sweat. They didn't like that.

'You'll have to put this on now,' said the one with the baby face. He held a blindfold limply in front of me. When I say blindfold I mean one of those velvet masks that I associate with beauty sleep and hangovers.

'I don't wear velvet,' I said. 'It brings me out in a rash.'

'For God's sake, do as you're told,' said baby face in a weary, mocking tone.

He was too young to have a weary, mocking tone. I stuck a thumb up under his jaw-bone. I rammed it up there so hard it blocked his windpipe and made him gag.

'Don't get smart with me, sonny,' I told him. 'I'm having a difficult time here.'

The one with the shaving cream on his ear snatched the mask from his companion's hand, at the same time cautioning him against any kind of retaliation. Then he looked to me with his big brown eyes and gave a little sour grin.

'Let's make it easy, shall we?' he said.

They hadn't doped me, coshed or cuffed me, so I let him pull the thing over my eyes.

'You just relax now,' he said patting my hand. 'Shan't be long.'

I tried to do as he bid. I tried to relax. I kept my mouth shut. I remained perfectly still. I let the blood warm my muscles. When the time came for me to move I didn't want to be stiff. I wanted the longest reach possible. I wanted to be able to tumble. I knew about tumbling.

They took the mask off in a lift. The lift was a small, primitive contraption with dark stained wood panels and an expanding grille. It creaked as we ascended at a painfully slow rate. I could tell from the sound of a speeding car that the building was located in a narrow street.

The man who met us on the top floor greeted me with a firm handshake and an apology. He wanted to start with an apology. He saw the mask hanging from the pocket of one of my new pals.

'Oh for God's sake, you didn't blindfold the man, did you?' he demanded.

'Well, we thought—'

'Go on – clear off.' He turned to me directly. 'I'm so sorry, Mister Fielding – Harry, if I may.'

He had established that he had my full name. Why was I thinking that hereafter he would avoid using any part of it?

He introduced himself. This was Hamilton's boss. The head of the firm.

'Idiots,' he muttered when the lift began its descent. 'Can't undertake a simple task without drawing attention to themselves.'

He pointed me towards a room across the landing. The room was furnished sparsely. It was lit by the main light, a yellowing bulb in a cheap shade. Not flat, not office, not hotel room. Something of all three. There was a small kitchen and a bedroom. The doors to both were open but the rooms were in semi-darkness. There were no personal effects to be seen. A thick blanket of dust unified the surfaces and the space. Nobody lived in these chambers. If this was an office it was used by somebody who had a lot of thinking to do, or phonecalls to make. There were no files, no papers, no computer.

The old man put me sitting on a hard chair in front of his desk. The chair he sat in behind the desk was one in which he felt uncomfortable, but he was at ease with this discomfort. He flicked cigarette ash from the V-necked pullover he wore under his suit, then he offered me a drink. He made no move that might have indicated where he kept the alcohol and the glasses. I could see no ashtray. The ashtray must have been hidden in the same place as the alcohol.

I declined his offer of a drink.

'Oh, sorry,' he said, 'I thought you liked whiskey.'

'What's happening here?' I asked.

He apologized again. I think he knew that his apologizing bothered me. His apologetic manner gave way suddenly. He sat stiffly in his chair pressing the tips of his fingers together. Here was an old man who wanted to unload his secrets. I took it that this, too, was a performance.

He gave me a memo to read. He had a copy of it himself. He kept pace with me as I read. The memo was from Hamilton. It was nearly three years old. I was the subject of this memo. It was a brief appraisal of my character, background and skills. *Not suitable* Hamilton had written at the end of it in his own hand. That is to say, I was not recruitment material for the service. Hamilton had interviewed me himself. He had been very positive. He had said that there was room for an ambitious fellow with a steady nerve. The report I now read described me as a 'trouble-maker who takes a good snap'.

'Good shot, too, by all accounts,' came the voice from across the desk. 'The man you shot in China-town – he deserved what he got, I take it?'

He had looked up from the memo. He was staring at me blankly. It was the kind of blank stare I had failed to master myself.

'Yes,' I said.

'Self-defence?'

'Protecting the innocent.'

He ignored the bitter cynicism in my voice.

'Jolly good.'

He glanced at a second report. There was no copy of this on offer.

'Chinese . . . from Hong Kong, yes?'

'As far as I know.'

'Well, that's a blessing, isn't it?'

'Is it?' I asked, but of course, there was no answer.

'I have a job for you. Nothing violent, you under-stand.'

Where had I heard that before?

'It's just I need an ambitious fellow who can take a good snap. Somebody who clearly can't be part of the firm. You'll be working directly to me. Nobody else will be involved. Payment to be arranged. Do you understand?'

'I understand.'

'First, of course, you'll have to spend a little time abroad – until we get this Chinatown business out of the way.'

I could only assume that the old man knew that I had been doing Hamilton's dirty work and that he was going to squeeze me until he got what he wanted to know out of me.

I looked at him with my best blank stare as he danced the fingers of one hand on his chin. What I now saw was the face of a man with a long record of defeats.

'I understand,' I repeated. It was a perfectly good lie. I wasn't about to elaborate.

Part 4

TWISTED

CHAPTER 11

THE CROOKED MILE

Dogs sprang from darkened doorways and from amidst the rubble as we drove the trucks through the deserted villages as fast as we dared. They would chase us, barking and snapping viciously at the wheels. These were the pets left behind in the evacuation. These dogs had reverted to being wild. They hunted in packs. Some of the larger animals would fling themselves at the driver's cab. You could hear their claws scratching at the door for an instant. They would come up again and again.

It wasn't the wild dogs that we feared. We were afraid of sniper fire, mortar rounds, landmines. Drivers washed down their trucks when they could. You wanted that white paint screaming under the big black letters that read UN. You wanted starch in that blue flag.

One volunteer driver had a little shrine of religious gewgaws in his cab. His wife had helped him install this in the depot in London. Another driver played cassette tapes continuously. A third sang songs he thought he had forgotten. Most of us just kept our mouths shut and our eyes on the tail of whatever was in front of us. I don't know about the others, but I ignored the marauding dogs. I acknowledged each body that I saw. I see you, I would say. I have made a note of where you lie. I will tell people where they can find you.

I prayed that if the convoy was to draw fire everything thrown at us would fall short. I prayed that if somebody was to be hit it would be somebody behind me, not in front. If some bastard in front of me was going to get killed at the wheel of his truck I prayed that by some miracle the dead man would keep his hands on the wheel and his foot on the accelerator.

I was an understrapper again. This time I got to travel abroad. Understrapper and killer hiding in Bosnia. My new boss was looking after me just as the old one had done, but this was a new phase for me. To survive was to be promoted. I only had to look out through my windscreen to see how grateful I should be for that.

I drove a truck full of milk powder. This made up for one of the two shots I had fired into the Chinaman's chest. This was a new phase in my protecting the innocent. Bringing sacks of milk powder to people made me want to weep like the drunk with his burst sack of coal.

Potter, the man responsible for doing deals with warlords and militiamen, was an Englishman. Potter was a different class of public school twerp to the ones with whom I was familiar. He was an outsider. A loner. This one would have confidently ended every school composition with the phrase 'And that was that'.

Potter was a military man comfortable out of uniform, a big-engined chap who secretly negotiated the amount of relief supplies that were to be surrendered to ensure safe passage for the rest. That is, if anyone was prepared to negotiate.

None of the drivers knew how much was getting through. We could only guess. We didn't talk about the deals that were made. We liked to think that somebody had calculated how much would be taken en route, based on previous demands, and had compensated for this. No doubt Potter sent memos to the Ministry of Defence in Whitehall advising as to the situation on the ground. I expect he wrote character sketches of individual warlords, mayors and other local power-brokers. I didn't like Potter. He reminded me of Hamilton.

The displacement of people had led to the proliferation of moving boundaries that had to be crossed and recrossed. Relief supplies were reaching the frightened and confused old people who had been put in the tourist hotels on the Adriatic coast. They were reaching refugees who had beds in shelters with numbers chalked on the floor. Individuals, families, whole villages could be lost. Names, numbers, map references mattered now as never before.

I didn't belong among these desperate people. Mine was a different kind of desperation. The tawdry interiors of charity shops upset me deeply. How could I cope with the misery that I found here?

I made promises to the lost people lying on the roadside. I ignored their wild dogs. I kept my eyes on the tail of the truck in front of me.

The convoy was stuck on a ridge, exposed to the surrounding mountain woods. We had crawled up the zig-zag road on the face of a butte. Around the bend ahead of me the steep descent into the valley began. There was a river in a gorge. The river skirted the butte. It rumbled beneath us like a ship's engine. The convoy had been stopped by militiamen on the far side of the butte. They had set up a roadblock at the bridge on the river. It was cold. The militiamen stamped their feet. The ones without gloves periodically blew into one hand, transferred their weapon to that hand, then blew into the other. The ones with gloves had got them from factories or farms. They were made of thick materials. These men either chose not to wear them on duty or had cut the index finger off. They felt safer with a naked finger in the trigger loop.

The ground was frozen hard. These were treacherous roads. When the negotiations were done the trucks would descend one at a time and cross the bridge into the next valley. In the meantime, each driver sat in his cab purposefully slumped over the steering wheel. The engines were kept running at first. It gave the impression that we were about our business and fully expected to pass through their road-block without undue delay. That couldn't be kept up for long, of course. Fuel had to be conserved.

Fletcher, the driver behind me, got into my cab. His heater was broken.

'You don't mind,' he said in his thick Glaswegian accent as he pulled the door closed behind him, 'it's just, ayh, there's no point in dying of exposure.'

I could see that he was embarrassed to ask this favour. He struck me as a man who usually got what he wanted. I suspected that most encounters that were not confrontational in nature embarrassed him. Clearly, that was no deterrent. Fletcher was a quick-tempered man. He had kicked up a fuss at the Austrian border over forms that we had been given to fill out. These forms were the size of newspapers. Potter had taken him to task and Fletcher had taken a swing at Potter. He could share my heater any time.

Ever since Hamilton had pulled me free of the Lisa Talbot affair I had been forced to live in the present exclusively. I had fooled myself into thinking that I could contribute just what suited me to Hamilton's little enterprise. I had believed that I could take a rational view of events and plan my escape. In fact, I had merely reacted to the immediate crisis by doing as I was told. I liked to think that I was putting into action the bones of an escape that I had carried with me ever since I had done my first job for Hamilton. Who was I trying to fool? There was no denying that it was Hamilton who had put me in Bosnia. If it wasn't to be Bosnia it would have been another war zone, some hell-hole in Africa.

Hamilton liked to think that he could always find

a place for a person, whatever their predicament. War zone, holiday camp, brothel, morgue, whatever suited him best. In Hamilton's world safe often meant safely preoccupied. An adept manipulator is a good judge of how his victim functions and what it takes to fill his plate.

The firm wasn't running any part of the relief operation. Hamilton simply ensured that I was given a job driving a truck. He wanted me at a safe distance, but retrievable. He wanted me fully preoccupied with the immediate dangers of relief convoy work in a war zone. He wanted me alive. I was still of use to him. No doubt he was convinced that should a stray bullet make a hole in my head he could find another Harry. I wasn't in the business of proving him wrong.

'You'll have time to think,' he had said to me just before I left London, 'time to put things in perspective.'

Even as the words came out of his mouth I knew that would be the kind of thinking a rat does in a wheel. It wasn't perspective I needed. I had these flashes that provided a grand view from a dizzy height. What I needed was a future, and I needed to work out what I had to do to get it. That was altogether a different kind of planning.

Sitting in that truck on that exposed ridge, I realized I had done nothing more than glance over my shoulder between those giddy flashes. I had survived thus far because it suited somebody else. I had devised no plan that would take account of the damage that had been done. I had suppressed my anger so that I might tumble forwards with slack muscles. In doing so I would present a difficult target.

Now that we were halted on this ridge, that bend in the road, that steep descent into the valley, seemed to hold special significance for me. I had a strong sense of foreboding. I had hurtled towards this point in my life to find that I could hardly bear to be stationary for a moment longer. I was in a hurry. The next encounter was an obstacle to the one that followed. I was hurrying towards some great and significant act, some calamitous gesture – I did not know which.

'Make you sick, wouldn't it?' said Fletcher.

'What? – yes. It would.'

There was a long silence between us, then Fletcher spoke again.

'See my brother, he's getting married on Saturday.'

'Is he?'

'Aye. The girl he's marrying, she's got steel ribs and a pin in her hip. They were in a crash. Both badly injured. I think that's why they're getting married. Can I ask you a question?'

'Ask.'

'Does that make sense to you?'

'Yes,' I said.

'They weren't right for each other – not before the crash . . .'

'Did you tell your brother that?' I asked.

A slow creeping grin appeared on his face.

'I better give him a call to wish them the best,' he said. 'Where did they say we could make calls?'

'They didn't say.'

'Aye, well, if you hear from any of these bastards you'll tell me. I have until Saturday.'

I said that I was sure he would be able to make his call.

There was another long silence between us. The fumes from the trucks spread around us and drifted upwards on the still air. The engines coughed and spluttered. The convoy no longer threw out a single body of noise. Alert and anxious, Fletcher looked out across the gorge at the trees beyond. I studied this stranger's face. I saw his fear. There was nothing wrong with the heater in his truck.

I wanted to show him that I, too, was afraid. I had never before wanted to reveal my fear. I had always sought to conceal it.

I said nothing. I sat there, my hands tightly gripping the steering wheel. I saw Maureen's frightened face on the beach in our cold paradise. I saw Jimmy with his open mouth standing in his office doorway. I saw Vinnie come out of the flames of his hotel. I was angry with my friends for having been afraid. It was the same anger the death of a friend could engender. It made no sense.

One of our escort, the same one who had reported the road-block at the bridge, approached.

'Engines off, please. Engines off.'

'Christ,' said Fletcher.

There was no point in asking how long the negotiations would take. If they weren't going to let us through it would be hell to have to turn back. There was no room to turn on this ledge. The trucks would have to descend into the valley to assemble for the humiliating return journey, a journey made more dangerous by having a full load.

I switched off my engine. Fletcher got out of the cab and returned to his own vehicle. He switched off his engine. Soon, all the engines had been cut. Now, there was just the sound of the river beneath us.

'Bastards,' I heard Fletcher shout as he conspicuously checked his load. He pulled hard on the ropes. He pushed and poked the goods. He got up on top of his load and stood with his fists on his hips. His eyes scoured the woods on the far side of the gorge.

'Bastards,' he shouted.

When he was finished he got back into his own cab and stayed there. In my wing mirror I could see the red hair on top of his head. He had put his head down on the steering wheel.

We were stuck on that ridge for twelve hours. The captain was sure that we could get through and so he persisted. When the captain stepped aside Potter performed. Naturally, both men flattered the local commander. They credited him with more power and influence than his rank demanded. Twelve hours was a long time to grip a steering wheel. Twice, we were ordered to start our engines. Twice, we were ordered to switch off. Twice, I sprang out of the cab and made my way to the bend in the road.

Twelve hours was long enough to be thinking about how I might see as far as Saturday. I had to slap my head. I had to remind myself that I was a selfish bastard with a truck full of milk powder to deliver. When I had made this delivery I would seize control of my life again. Somehow, I would set things right.

In pale, cold light I began my descent. It had taken me some time to get used to driving a truck. I had learnt early to keep the driver's door open on a steep gradient in terrain such as this. A runaway truck with a full load didn't make allowances for its former driver.

I applied gentle pressure to the brake and felt the weight behind me. There was little space on either side of the truck. The gorge to my left, rock face to my right. The lead escort and some five trucks had gone before me. In some spots the frozen ground was breaking up under the weight. I picked up speed. The river had begun to roar at my open door. I could feel its damp spray on my face, or was it cold air chilling my sweat that I felt? It was difficult to keep an even pressure on the air brakes. The truck began to rock. The surface of the dirt road became bumpy. The steering wheel shuddered. I could afford to go a little faster, I decided. It was one long curve to the bottom. Whatever about the narrowness and the surface of the road, its curve was easy to judge if nothing untoward happened. I hit a rough patch on the road and the rocking got worse. I tried to break its momentum by slowing. I could see myself bursting through the road-block and crossing the bridge. Near the bottom

I must have hit a boulder. I slammed on the brakes. The tail of the truck slid gracefully out to meet the rock face before bouncing to my left. I had hit a second boulder. In any case, I lost control. On my left the river emerged from the gorge to cut across the flat land in front of me. The men on the bridge could see this truck was in trouble. Were they going to move? They hesitated. The tail of the truck had lurched back into line. I glanced at my open door. It was swinging wildly on its hinges. I hesitated. There seemed to be a chance of recovery. By the time I had reached the bridge I had successfully compensated for the rocking and the swaying. I had reduced speed. Unfortunately, I misjudged the width of the truck. I clipped the nearside girder of the bridge. That was enough to cause the truck to ditch in the river.

I must have been thrown free instantly. There is a gap in my memory between the truck bursting through the rail and my swallowing a lot of water. I felt the force of the current. It had me pinned against rocks. I heard voices and I saw the river turn to milk. Then, a black hole opened up before me and I tumbled into it. It was a familiar blackness. Ideal for a tumbler. I remember thinking that this was the perfect end to my sordid odyssey.

I should have been thinking about my family and friends who had suffered because of the madness that had afflicted me. I should have been thinking about the milk powder lost in the river. Instead, I was thinking about Lisa Talbot. People like Lisa Talbot and me have a piece missing. There is a blind spot in our humanity. Often, people like us are in the best position to protect another. We are guardian angels with clipped wings.

Lisa was looking in the window at me. She was watching me tumble in my brightly lit room. She had her big unblinking eyes fixed on me. She was making that whistling noise through her teeth. She had never been afraid of me. I could see that now. We belonged together, like Fletcher's brother and his wife-to-be.

My angel with clipped wings reached a hand towards me. I could feel its warmth before we touched. When we touched I would straighten out of my tumble. I would take her hand. We were going to step through curtains in Chinatown. Yes, I was going to put things right.

Alas, there was no window. I was being held in the cold storage room of a meat factory. The refrigeration unit had been switched off when there was no meat left to hang on the hooks. I was lying on a damp army cot. There were five other cots set up with their heads against the wall. They were not occupied. Each had a single blanket and top sheet folded into a square on the canvas. The smell of animal blood hung heavily in the air. At first I couldn't move. I was trapped inside what felt like a cement waistcoat. I had broken ribs on my left side. My torso was bandaged tightly. So, too, was my left elbow. The pain in my chest was severe. Darts of pain passed through my eyeballs as they swivelled to take in my surroundings.

The angelic presence I had felt turned out to be Fletcher. There was some commotion on the other side of the steel door, then he came into the room with two militiamen. One of the militiamen introduced himself as a doctor. He spoke good English. He translated for the other one, the local commander.

'Your friend is allowed to visit,' he said, translating. 'You are lucky to be alive,' he added himself. He set about examining me. He was quite rough with his hands. 'The young man you hit is alive, but not so lucky,' he said after a brief silence.

'What – who did I hit?' I asked.

'You hit a soldier on the bridge, ya blind bastard,' interjected Fletcher. Fletcher was standing back, shifting from foot to foot.

The commander launched into an account of the militiaman's injuries. The doctor translated in a voice devoid of emotion.

'This is temporary,' he said when eventually the commander had ceased. Initially, I took it that he was referring to the way I had been corseted in bandages. Then, I caught the significance in his voice. 'Temporary,' he repeated, 'okay?'

What did he mean? Did he mean they were going to release me, or, did he mean they were going to take me to a proper prison?

'Okay,' I said. It wasn't okay. It was far from being okay.

'He wants you to rest comfortably,' he said, translating. 'There is talks with British representative. You – you can talk with your friend now.'

When the doctor had finished his examination he and the commander withdrew, leaving Fletcher standing incongruously in the middle of the room under two lines of meat hooks.

'Christ, man, look at you,' he blurted out. 'Potter's talking to some arsehole. It may be alright. The youngfella you hit – he's up and about,' he whispered nervously.

I had had enough help from the Potters of this world. I wanted out of this place on my own terms. I decided they wanted Fletcher to see that I was being well treated, and that I was being attended by a doctor. They were going to move me. This place wasn't secure. I could hear fighting in the distance.

I questioned Fletcher in a quiet, urgent voice. Where exactly were we? I was shocked to learn that the convoy had made its delivery – Fletcher was on his way back to the base with his empty truck. He couldn't stay long, he told me. Potter was doing his best for me, he said. So, too, was the captain.

'You've got to get me out of here,' I told him.

'Are you mad?' he said when he had looked first to the left, then to the right.

I got him to describe the scene immediately beyond the closed door. There were two guards. Boys in uniform.

'Just find a way to open the door,' I told him.

'I don't even know you,' he said. His voice got louder. He screwed up his face. 'No way, pal. I'm just here to wish you well.'

He handed me three bars of chocolate.

Yes. I must have been a little mad. Just what did I expect of this man? I could see how frightened he was and yet, he had come to visit me.

He brought me blankets from two of the unused cots.

'Here,' he said draping them over me. 'Aren't you cold? It's bloody freezing in this kip. There. That'll do you.'

I thanked him. I apologized. I told him my mind was addled.

That made him angry. His face flushed.

'We got the stuff through, anyway,' he said. There was a silence then he said, 'Don't you worry. I'll see to Potter. He'll see you right.'

He left abruptly.

It *was* Potter who got me out. He wouldn't tell me how he had done it. He would only say that I had put the whole convoy in jeopardy with my reckless driving. The soldier I had hit was in a bad way, he said. He told me this as he helped me into the back of a personnel carrier. He knew I felt bad about the lost milk powder and the truck, so he worked on that. He repeatedly remarked that it was 'a pity to have disappointed the people'.

I ate all three bars of chocolate myself, one after another.

I was going home in disgrace. Potter was the hero. It would all be in one of his reports. He *had* helped me, it was true. I should have been grateful, but I wasn't.

The wreck of the truck was still in the river when we passed over the bridge and began to climb the steep hill. Some time after that Potter pretended to forgive me. He enquired about my injuries. He said he would arrange to have a doctor look at me as soon as we reached the base. While he talked I whistled through my teeth.

God bless Lisa Talbot, I thought. God bless Fletcher.

CHAPTER 12

CUMULATIVE PROVOCATION

On the aeroplane bound for London I had an aisle seat across from the galley. There was some confusion over a batch of dinners.

'That's the chicken,' I was able to say to the hostess.

It was not my business to say anything, of course, but I was right about the batch being chicken.

'They're changing the system,' I told her. 'They're laying on new containers. That's what I've been told.'

She smiled, and that made me feel foolish. I handled my tray clumsily. I wanted a stiff drink. I took heart from these pathetic signs of what passed for normality in Harry Fielding's life.

I was hungry. I ate everything that was edible on the tray. I made a little ceremony of it. My patience had returned. The pain in my battered body reminded me that my sojourn in Bosnia was not a dream, but the pain would eventually cease.

When I had finished eating I ordered a double Scotch and picked up an English newspaper. On the bottom of the front page a brief article announced that the man arrested and tried for the London serial killings had been convicted on two counts of murder. He had been sentenced to two terms of life imprisonment. There had been sufficient evidence to convict in two cases. The police, however, had been unable to present incontrovertible evidence in the remaining cases. The convicted man would not admit to having murdered the others. The police had caught a murderer. Officially, they had not caught the serial killer. Officially, the files on the other victims would remain open; the hunt would continue.

I thought about Angela Richardson's family. I could see one of them visiting this man in gaol to ask him if he had killed their Angela. I could see the mute prisoner present a stony face when asked where he had put her body. I could see the family visiting the area where the shallow grave of his last victim had been discovered. I could see them – father, mother, uncles – probing the ground. It would be a long time before they were convinced that she was not buried there. They would never give up hope. They would look for her in the streets and on wasteland. Eventually, they would neglect to tell people what they were doing but would continue to believe that someday someone would tell them where Angela could be found.

I needed a shave. I had bought a packet of disposable razors at the airport. They were whistling in my inside pocket. I got up and went to the toilet thinking I might have to use the entire packet just to scrape my face clean.

I stood in front of the sink intent on studying my reflection. I presented my best blank stare.

Missus Lamb didn't see me enter the building. Had she seen me she would have come out to greet me. She made a point of greeting me if I was absent for a week or more. She was slipping. Perhaps she was going blind or deaf. Perhaps she was out shopping. I had forgotten that people went out to shop. Perhaps my forgetfulness was the cause of the razors whistling irritatingly in my pocket.

A note from Maureen had been slid under my door. I took it into the kitchen. I sat down in front of the wellington boots to read it. The note was written on a small piece of paper that had been torn from a desk pad and put in a business envelope. The paper smelt vaguely of coconut. That was her smell. There were a few lines to tell me she had lost her job, and that she could be reached at the Amsterdam number she had given me. She would be there for a short time in any case. There was nothing more.

I got up and went into the living room. I stood in the middle of the floor clutching Maureen's note. The light on the answering machine was flashing. My brother had telephoned. Our father had had an operation. As a result, his health was much improved. My brother and his wife were anxious that I come to dinner. My niece wanted to visit me in my flat. The message was a month old. There had been other calls. A string of them. No messages had been left. There was just the tone.

I went to my tower. I checked the street for lingering strangers. Everybody was moving one way or another.

I poured myself a drink on my way back to the kitchen. In the kitchen I sat down again in front of the boots. I listened to the fridge for five minutes or more, then I opened its door. Some small thing had crawled into one corner to die. It had turned blue. There was nothing else in there. Just cold air.

I finished my drink in the bathroom. The billiard-ball caught my eye. I had forgotten that somebody could be as old as Missus Lamb. Perhaps she was in hospital. Perhaps she was dead.

I knocked on the wall with the billiard-ball. The wait was longer than ever before, but I did get a reply. She knocked heavily on the wall. It was an affirmative knock. She shouted something. I couldn't make out what she said, but I was happy to hear her muffled voice. I let out a small, joyful sound.

Freddie was charming. Freddie could be boorish. Freddie was loud. That is not to say that Freddie was indiscreet. He was never indiscreet.

He was surprised to get an invitation to my flat. It didn't bother me to have him call at the flat in this instance. It was the last night I would be spending there. He turned up with an expensive bottle of wine.

'Harry, old boy,' he boomed in the doorway, 'this is an honour.'

'Get in,' I told him.

He cast a critical eye about the room.

'Well, well,' he said mildly.

'What have you got there?' I asked, indicating the bottle.

He passed me the bottle with his eyebrows raised.

'Come into the kitchen,' I said.

He followed me closely.

'Don't sit on that. Sit there.'

I reached down two glasses. He saw that my body was stiff.

'You look well, Harry. Now me, I need more exercise. I need a holiday. The kids want to go to Spain. I don't want to go to Spain.'

I opened the bottle and poured.

'You can fit more in that glass,' he said holding his out in front of him.

At that point Missus Lamb knocked on my door.

'You're back,' she said when I opened the door. She was glad to see me, but there was a reproachful note in her voice. She was more frail than I remembered; not so frail, however, that she couldn't push her way into my flat.

I introduced her to Freddie. Freddie poured her a glass of wine and made a fuss over her.

'Don't sit there, Missus Lamb,' he said, 'come into the living room.'

His loud voice and facial expressions encouraged

her. He shared a joke with her at my expense. Missus Lamb much appreciated that. It won her trust.

She told Freddie that she wanted me to rearrange the stored items in her flat.

Yet again.

Freddie immediately undertook to do the job. He was speaking for both of us without consultation.

Missus Lamb was surprised. When could we do it, she wanted to know.

'Now, of course,' said Freddie plunging his hands into the pockets of his tweed trousers. 'That is, if it suits you.'

She was thrilled, and also a little anxious. After all, she didn't really need the items to be shifted. It was an excuse to have company.

I gave a look that said, you fraud, Freddie.

The eyebrows went up.

It was best that we get it over with as soon as possible. I led the way to her flat directly. She was apologetic. She could only offer us tea and biscuits.

When we had finished rearranging the furniture and belongings Freddie insisted that he get us an Indian take-away meal. It would be his treat. Missus Lamb readily agreed. She wanted Freddie to order for her.

While Freddie was out getting the food Missus Lamb prepared the table in her kitchen.

'Come on, Harry,' she said, 'fill the kettle. Fred will be back and the tea won't be ready. Tea is the right thing with an Indian dinner, don't you think?'

She went on to complain about the new tenant,

the one occupying Lisa Talbot's flat. A single gent; altogether too smart, too eager to please, in her estimation.

I was looking around me. What could I give her? I wanted to give her something from my flat, even if she had no more room. I could think of nothing I had that she would want. Best to leave her the keys. She could clear it out as it suited her before the landlord let it.

I had a picture in my mind of a billiard-ball in the corner of an empty room.

The Indian dinner was a big success. Freddie made a point of taking an interest in Missus Lamb's family photographs. When we had finished in Missus Lamb's flat Freddie and I went out to his car.

'There,' he said, putting it in my hand, 'a fine piece of work. A little heavier than the Beretta, of course. Eight in the clip. You asked for one of these . . .' he produced a compatible silencer, '. . . now this was a bugger to get.'

I sat in my darkened tower and I thought about Freddie. He wasn't like any of the others. He could never be one of the Georges. If he was like anybody he was like me. Were it not that Freddie's work required complete detachment, I might have been foolish enough to confide in him. Now here lay a significant difference between us. It would never have entered Freddie's mind to confide in me. Freddie always liked the other fellow to feel safe. He didn't want to burden him with an unnecessary intimacy. I had learnt much from him. I had studied the ease with which he moved. Good people can get tired of doing the right thing. People like Freddie and me have the patience they lack, even if we don't have the scruples.

Freddie would survive us all. With that thought my stomach began to ache. I went out to the local cafeteria. It was late. They would be closing in half an hour. The dishwasher had been let off early. He had his coat on, but he was sitting in one of the cubicles, smoking. He was in his late thirties. His face was hard and shiny. He was looking out the window at the people passing in the street. Anyone glancing in at him would have seen that he was an unhappy man. His set expression begged a question. How could he have done better for himself?

'Go home, Billy,' the owner called to him.

Billy answered with a lame, dismissive wave of the hand.

The owner took my order with a grunt.

I had talked to Billy once. He couldn't have been earning much money dishwashing. A little more, perhaps, than he would have got on the dole. This didn't matter. He would have taken a pay cut without complaining had the boss told him business was slack. It wouldn't have occurred to Billy that he was washing the same number of dishes. Tonight, he was working towards a different facial expression, a frown that said he was sure he would find a way to escape this wretched existence, that he would better himself just as soon as he could see that way.

He began to laugh quietly to himself. He bunched his shoulders. He pulled hard on his cigarette, then he extinguished it in the ashtray with a vigorous rubbing motion. Then, he got up and left.

I acknowledged him with a twitch of the head as he passed. He replied with the same grunt his boss had offered.

While I ate I went through the mental list of tasks I had set myself. The car was ready. It had a full tank of petrol. I had made arrangements regarding the money I had left. It was not a large sum, but it would be enough for three months or more.

I didn't like carrying a gun loose. I had no holster for the gun I had purchased from Freddie. Freddie had had no suitable holster to give me. Had I had the holster for the Beretta I might have been able to modify that. The police, however, had taken it from me. When they saw the holster they had got very keen. It was as if they had found a second gun.

'Is that alright?' the owner asked from behind the counter. His tone suggested that he had expected me to complain.

'Yes,' I said. 'Thank you.'

He grunted.

The minister was spending Sunday in the country. The police at the entrance to the estate were suspicious of me in my blue van. I gave my name as Barrett. I told them I was expected, but that I was early. They asked for means of identification. I showed them a driver's licence in the name of Barrett. They called the house. The minister instructed that I was to be admitted.

I drove the van into the courtyard. One of the minders discreetly photographed me from his car. No doubt they would give the van a thorough inspection while I was in the house. A check on the registration would only reveal that I was not the owner, nothing more. I could be confident that the listed owner's name would arouse no suspicion. One minder politely asked to look in the bag I was carrying before I left the courtyard. None of this scrutiny was of consequence now.

The minister introduced me to his wife. She reminded him that we had already met. He blew his nose, led me into his study and locked the door.

'What are you doing here?' he asked with a coldness that was understandable in the circumstances.

I passed him the bag I was carrying. It contained his wellington boots.

'You'll be needing these,' I said.

He took the boots out of the bag and placed them at the side of his desk. He folded the bag and handed it to me.

I pointed to the telephone. 'Call Hamilton,' I said. 'Tell him Barrett has contacted you. He has sent you photographs. Tell him you must see him. Tonight.'

'Don't play games with me,' the minister warned.

I recited Hamilton's number.

'What photographs are these?' he asked. 'Why should Hamilton come here in the middle of the night?'

'He'll come,' I assured him. Again, I pointed to the telephone.

'Why?'

'You're valuable to him now. You're part of the team.'

'I'll not play your games.'

'You really should ring him and discuss the matter.'

'Are you threatening me?'

He was standing directly in front of me now, as though he were barring my way.

'Ask Hamilton,' I said.

'What photographs?' he demanded.

'Ask him,' I said, trying to maintain the same even voice.

He offered no response. He made the silence that followed his own. His eyes searched me for cracks.

'He'll not come,' he said eventually. 'He'll not come because I'll not be inviting him.'

'You should do this for an old pal,' I said, 'for somebody who has helped you out of a jam, Minister.'

He pointed to the door. I showed him a print struck from one of the set of negatives I had given Hamilton. This was the first the minister knew of these pictures. It must have come as a hell of a shock. The photographs Alex Simson had sent him were of little consequence compared to this.

'There's more,' I told him.

He looked at me, then he backed away slowly and turned to his desk. This slowness was his way of warning me that I was going to regret my actions. The control he had over his facial muscles clearly did not extend to his fingers. I told him what to say as he dialled. His was a slow, deliberate dialling. I spoke rapidly. While he waited for a reply he lit a cigar. He kept his eyes fixed firmly on my face while he spoke into the mouthpiece.

He gave a good performance. Hamilton agreed to meet. If there was bad news Hamilton liked to get it first-hand. He also liked to run a mercy mission. It usually meant that he got his claws in deeper.

Hamilton would be galled. He would be outraged. Harry Fielding had not learnt his lesson. When Hamilton had the details of this crude, freelance attempt at blackmail he would take 'executive action'. Harry would become one of the missing people.

The damn rooks were croaking in the branches above me. Before I cut across to my vantage point on the rise I took two pebbles from the river and put them in my mouth. I turned them slowly with my tongue. This had a soothing effect. I had a long wait ahead of me. I had to remain alert. Where once I panicked I was now patient. Fretting drained a body's energy. It made a person listless. It made them less vigilant. Aside from the security in the immediate vicinity of the house and at the gate there was an occasional patrol through the outer reaches of the estate.

I had parked the van in a secluded spot beyond

the estate wall. I had recovered the gun from its hiding place. I had a clear view of the house and the rough path between the rise and the river. I had my two smooth pebbles. The arrangement was simple enough. The minister would slip away from the house to rendezvous with Hamilton at the appointed hour. This was a meeting that could not wait. Neither of them wanted to be seen together, certainly not at two o'clock in the morning, not if one of them were somehow to be linked to the disappearance of Angela Richardson, not if they were to be of use to each other in the future. Hamilton was to enter the estate at a given point. He was to climb the wall and follow the river due east to where it skirted the rise. The river was shallow. He could cross with ease. He was to cross here and wait on the rough path by the river bank. He was to be careful to avoid the police patrol.

The birds stopped croaking. The wind picked up. It grew dark. There was intermittent moonlight. The damp earth beneath my feet filled my nostrils with a pungent smell. I listened for the car, that I was sure would stop short of earshot. I listened for the sound of men advancing on the rough path, though I knew I would not hear them approach with this wind.

The bandage around my torso had loosened, but my aching ribs served only to remind me of my survival thus far, and of my recuperative powers. I felt acutely the remotest stirring in my surroundings. I felt the planet spinning. To a man with a gun in his hand everything looks like a target. I stood by a tree slowly turning the two stones in my mouth.

Hamilton arrived first. I saw him wade through the shallow water. He didn't seem to mind getting his feet wet. It was as if he didn't notice they were wet. I watched him patrol a length of path. His demeanour suggested that it was he who had called the meeting. Though the length of path remained in my field of vision, he repeatedly disappeared when the moon was momentarily obscured by fast-moving clouds. He made no attempt to observe the house. He was content to remain at the appointed spot. He had no doubt that this was the meeting place. Though the minister was late Hamilton looked at his watch just once, then he put his hands in the pockets of his camel-hair coat. He surveyed his surroundings, but in a covert manner. His apparent contentment with the way things stood no doubt was intended to unsettle anyone who might be watching. It suggested that he was aware of their presence and had planned accordingly.

When the minister eventually came into view I removed the stones from my mouth and quietly made my way down onto the path. I emerged at a point some five yards behind Hamilton. When Hamilton turned he kept his hands in his coat pockets. So did I. Hamilton stood his ground. The minister and I converged. We both halted a little more than arm's length from him. Hamilton didn't speak at first. He just stared at me. Finally, he turned to the minister.

'Well, Minister,' he said, 'you were telling me of your difficulties.'

The stubble on the minister's chin was oddly disconcerting. It was out of character. This small oversight suggested that he might do something rash.

'Your friend, here,' said the minister to Hamilton, 'he's playing games.'

Hamilton turned again to me, this time in mock surprise.

'Really?' he said. 'Is this true, Harry?'

Some narrow their eyes to show that they are shrewd. Not Hamilton. He had the large, sullen eyes of a tyrant. I had seen those eyes in my father's head.

'Always getting into trouble, what?' he said. He turned to the minister. 'What does he want?' he asked.

'I don't quite see the point of this,' came the reply. 'I'm to ask you, apparently.'

Hamilton looked to me again.

'I want his help,' I said.

'Financial?' he asked.

'No.'

'Ah.'

'You see, Minister,' I said, 'I'm in trouble. I shouldn't have got involved.'

'What do you want from me?' the minister demanded. 'Why is he here?' he asked, indicating Hamilton. 'Hamilton,' he said, 'I thought you had control of the situation.'

'I've had to let this man go,' Hamilton replied. 'He shot a man in Chinatown. He's a danger to us all.'

The minister didn't give a damn what I had done in Chinatown.

'Have you brought the photographs?' he asked me.

Hamilton took one hand out of one pocket. He raised a finger and interjected. 'You see before you, Minister, a man with a grievance. He must now tell us what he wants otherwise we will get no sleep tonight. He must make his proposal. He must tell me what it is I can do. If it's a job you want, Harry, or a pension, you can have neither.' He spoke without bitterness or doubt. He gave one of his thin smiles.

They were standing beside each other now, bearing down on me. I looked to the minister.

'The man in Chinatown,' I said, 'I shot him because he was beating his wife.' I pulled a finger out of my pocket and pointed it at Hamilton. 'This man has caused grievous harm to people who matter to me,' I said.

'Oh come now,' said Hamilton as though genuinely searching for the roots of a terrible misunderstanding.

My face must have darkened for the minister glanced anxiously to Hamilton.

'One way or the other, people get more than they deserve, don't you think?' I asked them both.

I shot Hamilton twice with the silenced pistol that I drew from my other pocket.

The minister's face gave a little twitch. His eyes smarted. The shock made him take a step backwards, but he didn't run. Even in his state of shock he was appraising my act, defining it as a solution. He was measuring the distance between himself and the entity on the ground. He was answering questions, not passing judgement.

I reminded him that he was here to help. I made him carry the body with me. We got it across the river and over the wall. I had misjudged the spot. We came out of the estate some three hundred yards short of the point I had intended. We were forced to carry the body along a country lane for the three hundred yards, then cross into the woods on the far side. There were another two hundred yards to the van.

I reminded the minister that he had wanted to know what had been done with Angela Richardson's body. I told him that he was about to find out. He accepted this. He understood that this was a punishment. In some strange way he had been seduced by the horror of what had just occurred, of what we were now doing. He had grasped that his role was that of accomplice. He had good reason to believe that we might get away with it. He was afraid of being caught, but he wanted to see this through. His soul was already damned. Here was a lesson in corruption from which he would learn much. It was an act of self-discovery. I felt him pushing from behind. He was more clumsy than me, but he kept pushing. He pushed when our way was lit by moonlight. He pushed when we were in the dark.

Hamilton had given the impression of carrying a gun, but there was no gun. He had driven down from London in the green Rover. When I had the body covered in the van I gave the minister Hamilton's car keys. I also gave him a cap and a pair of gloves to wear. I told him to follow in the Rover.

I set out for London. As the moon swung back and forth over the road I thought about what lay ahead of me. Then, I indulged in some idle speculation. If my new master had made me his understrapper so that I might inform on Hamilton's devious private enterprise and thereby protect him, I had, at least in part, accomplished that task. I had protected my master without his knowing it. There could be no more effective protection than that. In any case, he would never know. He would not see Hamilton or myself again.

I pulled over in a quiet residential street in Wandsworth. I kept the engine running. The minister pulled in a short distance behind me. I opened the passenger door of the van. He got out of the Rover and locked the door. He climbed into the van for the last leg of our journey. He said nothing at first. He stared straight ahead.

'What are you going to tell your wife?' I asked. 'How will you explain your absence?'

There was no reply.

'You don't want her thinking you're seeing another woman.'

No reaction.

'Somebody else is seeing my wife,' I said helpfully.

He kept staring straight ahead. He kept his mouth shut.

I changed the subject.

'When is your documentary on the television?' I asked.

'The end of next month,' he replied. 'The twenty-eighth.'

'That's nice,' I said.

'It will be broadcast at 7.50,' he said.

I looked at him for as long as I dared keep my eyes off the road.

As I drove towards the crematorium I wondered how I could have done better. I could have made a point of not getting involved. I realized that I had always striven to be involved. Intervention had at once been the thing that drove me and the core of my defence. In this respect I had been ambitious.

I was conscious of having performed a heinous act. My journey had taken me infinitely further than the mountains of Bosnia. I had witnessed a killing, I had photographed it, I had conspired to conceal the act, I had killed to protect a stranger. Finally, I had killed to protect those who had already been hurt. In my mind I could not separate these events.

Once again, I found myself thinking about Lisa

Talbot. Somehow, we, too, were inseparable. No doubt her counsel had advised her that the law of provocation would not assist with her plea to have her conviction for murder reduced to one of manslaughter. She had not been the victim of the repeated attacks. Even if she had been the victim the plea would have been ineffective. She had not retaliated immediately during a sudden, temporary loss of self-control.

I realized that Lisa and I were not given to fits. We could afford no regrets.

I have become one of the missing people, but I am very much alive. I look at prints I struck from the negatives I gave to Hamilton knowing that those prints prove nothing without the negatives. Without the negatives they are easily discredited. I read back to myself this account of my tumbling from grace and I find that it is much like one of Hamilton's memos, a testimony to misjudgement. I am conscious that I have no second life. I have, however, acquired a second pair of eyes. With these eyes I can, at last, see my true self. Not a double, not an opposite, but rather a crooked man with jagged pieces missing. I can bend to any shape to escape. I can save myself. That is my one talent. Watch how the crooked man runs. See how he evades even the lookalike who would kill him. Watch how he finds a space no one else can fit in. He is not brave, but he is patient and he has a steady hand.